ALL OR NOTHING IN MAGIC CITY

ALL OR NOTHING IN MAGIC CITY

MAGIC CITY CHRONICLES™ BOOK EIGHT

TR CAMERON   MICHAEL ANDERLE   MARTHA CARR

For those who seek wonder around every corner and in each turning page. Thank you choosing to share the adventure with me. And, as always, for Dylan and Laurel.

— TR Cameron

THE ALL OR NOTHING MAGIC CITY TEAM

Thanks to the JIT Readers

Dorothy Lloyd
Wendy L Bonell
Larry Omans
Dave Hicks
John Ashmore

If I've missed anyone, please let me know!

Editor
Skyhunter Editing Team

CHAPTER ONE

Ruby traveled along the rooftops a few blocks southeast of the Strip, looking for trouble. She said, "Nothing here so far. What about you all?"

Her boyfriend, Demetrius, was the first to reply. "The drones don't have anything interesting, other than some drunk tourists wandering around." His eyes were all over the city, courtesy of a small horde of commercial drones that his advanced AI bots ran for him. They would alert him to any unexpected deviations from the norm, including but not limited to those related to overambitious alcohol consumption.

Her sister asked, "Are the tourists cuter than Jewel?"

As always, the mocking use of her callsign irritated Ruby. "Shut up, you. D, do *not* answer that."

Idryll, Ruby's companion, replied, "Nothing here in the south, either. Unless you want to count the pair of drunk dwarves singing an off-key duet. Frankly, that could be considered criminal, given the volume and the utter absence of skill."

Ruby laughed. "If a day ever passes when you don't have something to complain about, I'll be sure to mark it down on my calendar so we can celebrate each year. I'll record it in my journal for the sake of future *Mirra,* too. On this day, my companion did not complain once. So, there's hope."

The shapeshifter countered, "Anyone forced to spend as much time with you as I would be in a perennial bad mood, too. Frankly, I'm an absolute joy to be around, considering."

Morrigan replied, "Having grown up with you, I can verify the truthfulness of that statement. Also, nothing yet to the southwest, either. I wonder, will it be a quiet night in Magic City?"

Ruby said, "With friends like you, who needs the Paranoid Defense Agency?"

Idryll laughed. "At least we don't have to worry about them anymore."

Morrigan's voice was full of doubt. "I'm not sure of that."

Ruby paused to rest, perched on the edge of a building and surveying the street below. Anyone looking up would see a woman in black leather, with a dragon face mask and a sword hilt sticking up over her shoulder. They might also notice the bulletproof vest and the pistol on her thigh. Her other weapons, both arcane and not, were less obvious but at least as potent. "Andrews and his sidekick were afraid. I saw it in their eyes, both of them."

Idryll replied, "Scared of me, I'm sure."

Ruby smiled at the boast. "Who wouldn't be, really?"

Morrigan laughed and seemed about to say something when Demetrius broke in. "An alarm is going off at one of the power plants I monitor. It's directly south of the center of the Strip. Idryll's closest." He didn't talk about his work much, but Ruby knew he had gigs providing cybersecurity to a substantial number of businesses around town, including several industrial sites.

Morrigan asked, "Do we care? Last I checked, we weren't utility people."

Demetrius matched her sassy tone. "I think you might make an exception in this case. Internal cameras show the intruders are all Drow. There are a bunch of them. I'm sending drones down to get a better look."

Ruby had enabled the infomancer's drone fleet by hiring him through her family's casino, Spirits. She had a certain latitude, now that bringing Daphne into the business had proven to be lucrative, and she used that flexibility for all that it was worth. *Plus, since I'm still working there one day a week unpaid, it's almost fair.* She said, "Thank goodness. This patrol was getting downright boring. Glad to help out. Barb, can you get us there?"

Her sister replied, "Of course. I've been to all of them as part of my day job. You know, if you did any work, you might have portals to useful places, too."

While she waited for Morrigan to arrive, Ruby asked, "Any sign of the Hat?"

Demetrius laughed. "Is that his super villain codename now? The Hat?"

"Do you have anything better?"

After a pause, he replied, "Actually, I guess I don't. Anyway, no sign of the Drow in the fedora."

Idryll muttered, "That hat will be mine. Then I shall be known as the Hat."

A couple of minutes later, they were under cover outside the fence that protected the site. The plant was of the solar variety, and the central building was some distance away. Rectangular panels surrounded the structure to gather in the sun. Even the building's roof was covered with them, preventing their usual means of ingress. Ruby asked, "What do you remember?"

Morrigan cut a striking figure in the red cowl that complemented her magical mask and the impressive bow in her hand. She replied, "Pretty normal stuff. Huge building filled with lots of mammoth unfamiliar equipment, with tons of power lines running all over the place."

"It's not like a gas or oil plant, right? It's not particularly explosive, I mean."

Demetrius confirmed, "That's correct. There shouldn't be anything that would directly lead to an explosion in there. But there's a lot of electricity, which carries its own danger."

Idryll asked, "Who does this station supply?"

"It's the primary source of power for the Strip."

Morrigan sounded doubtful. "Really?"

Ruby could picture Demetrius nodding in what she considered his "professor" mode. He replied, "Really, really. If I remember right, the casino owners and the Council all have an ownership stake in the place. Lessens the possibility of someone extorting them for power, I guess."

She nodded. "That's on-brand. Pretty smart business decision too, especially if it's not particularly volatile, which lessens liability issues since they're inexpert in the field. So, let's get in there before the Drow start breaking important stuff."

She led her partners on a quick jog through the solar panels, moving in a slight crouch to stay below the tops of them. The lenses in her mask flipped automatically through scanning modes, looking for traps. She didn't expect to find any. The invaders had no real reason to place traps this far out unless the whole operation was one big ploy aimed at them, and she wasn't so arrogant as to think she rated *that* high on the local criminal element's to-do list. They reached the building without detecting any opposition, Morrigan fooling the cameras with her newly learned illusion trick. Ruby hadn't yet had time to get the details but knew that she was pretty good at spoofing visual sensing.

Her sister asked, "How do we want to play this?" Her bow had been in her fist from the moment they exited the portal, and the fingers on her free hand clenched and unclenched like she was limbering them for a speedier draw from the quiver at her back.

Ruby said, "Any more information from inside, D?"

He sighed. "No. I'm pretty sure they've got an info-mancer blocking me. The images I can access are too static to be trusted."

Ruby frowned. "As if they let us see they were in there, then cut off what they were doing?"

"Exactly as if."

Okay, maybe we're higher on that to-do list than I thought. Dammit. "We should assume they're ready for us. Still, let's go in quietly if we can."

Morrigan replied, "Given that there's only one door unless we want to try to enter through the loading docks, that's going to be difficult."

Idryll said, "I vote for the loading dock."

After a moment of thought, Ruby nodded. "Here's what we'll do. Barb, you stay here. When I call for it, make some noise, bang on the door, something. Then Cat and I will sneak inside."

Good-natured sarcasm dripped from her sister's words. "Wow, did you have to go to school to become such a brilliant strategist?"

Ruby replied, "Shut it," and ran with her partner at her heels. Upon arrival at the heavy garage door, she gestured for her companion to take the lead. The shapeshifter grew as she moved toward the garage door handle, her body bulking up but not losing its humanoid form. Ruby said, "Barb, go."

When the noisy distraction sounded from the front of the building, Idryll gave the handle a solid yank. The lock holding it broke, and she lifted the door. Ruby covered herself in illusionary invisibility and rolled inside as soon as there was space to do so. She came up in a defensive crouch, ready to fight.

The area was filled with crates on pallets, wooden boxes with stenciled letters and numbers that meant nothing to her, some of them partially covered by tarps. Sounds emanated from deeper into the building, and she caught a faint thermal signature to her left. She crept toward it, ready to attack, but discovered only a uniformed security guard lying on the floor unconscious. She checked his pulse, which didn't seem right. "Dammit. Downed security guard. Cat, see what you can do for him. Barb, get in here."

Another thermal plume was visible a dozen feet away,

and she approached under her veil. Ruby got behind the Drow sentry, who held a rifle in a position that indicated he knew how to use it. She slinked in close enough to discharge a dart into the back of his neck, then caught him before he could hit the floor and make noise as the tranquilizer overwhelmed his system. She dragged him out of the way, pleased with the success of that particular maneuver.

A minute later, laughter came from high above. *Male* laughter. The male laughter of the hat-wearing Drow. "Magic City's would-be heroes have arrived. I was beginning to think you wouldn't show up." Then, without changing his mocking tone, he said, "Beat them down."

CHAPTER TWO

"Well, hell," Ruby said. "All right. Spread out, do what you can, try not to kill anyone. Barb, unless you get up high, I doubt you'll be able to use your bow. And going up there probably makes you the most obvious target."

Her sister complained, "That's no fun. Magic it is. And knives."

Ruby rounded the corner, fully aware that a pair of enemies awaited her. She grabbed the pile of crates behind them with force magic and pulled it over, causing each of her foes to jump aside in opposite directions. She used more force magic to leap over the barrier she'd created and landed beside the first, a Drow woman who was already scrabbling to her feet encased in a protective sphere of shadow magic.

Ruby deemed herself close enough to trust her accuracy. She drew her pistol and fired at a downward angle. The anti-magic bullet penetrated the shield and continued through to break the other woman's shin. Her foe screamed, and her magical protection fell. A dart to her muscular bare arm took her out of the fight.

Idryll shouted a warning. Ruby dropped into a crouch and spun in time to see the shapeshifter tackle the other one of the pair, who'd been aiming a rifle at the back of her head. "Thanks, partner."

The shapeshifter's arm pistoned down, and a moment later the rifle went flying toward the open garage door. "No problem at all," she growled.

Demetrius said, "Did some research. The part of the company our folks don't own is in the hands of a human corporation. That didn't seem particularly problematic at first, but then I traced their corporate philanthropy. They've been giving money to politicians who have taken hard public anti-magical stances."

Ruby shook her head. "At least the Hat is consistent."

Demetrius gave a dark chuckle. "So, you're seriously going with that, then? No kidding? The Hat. Please take him out so I don't have to hear you say that name anymore."

She growled, "Count on it."

Morrigan crept forward with a knife in her off-hand and her main one empty. Her target faced away from her. She took him out without a fight, tapping him on the side of the neck with her stun knuckles. He fell awkwardly, and she failed to catch him, allowing him to land with a clatter.

An instant later, a second guard ran into view, already firing. Morrigan dove aside, cursing herself for not noticing the second of the pair. "Watch out. They seem to have decent discipline and are watching out for one another."

Confirmations came from her partners as she grabbed a pair of discs from her belt with her left hand. She raised her right arm and shot her grapnel up into the rafters. The tiny motor attached to the device lifted her, and she cast the grenades as soon as she was high enough to see over the obstructions. They discharged a second later, taking out a few more of the surrounding Drow.

A scrape from the side gave away another enemy, and her head snapped around, finding a rifle pointing up at her. Morrigan released the line, dropped to the floor, and threw herself sideways to hide behind the nearest stack of crates. "There are a lot of these jerks here."

Ruby replied, "Yeah, which makes you wonder where he got them. I thought we knocked him out of operation for at least a while after we took out all the people at the warehouse."

Idryll said, "Lots of Drow around on both planets. Maybe he has deeper connections with them than we assumed and used whoever was available as a matter of convenience before. Now we've forced him to turn to his people as a resource."

Morrigan rounded the next corner and discovered another pair of enemies waiting. She reached out with her magic and yanked on the rifle strap of the nearest, jerking the man forward and ruining his shot. That forced the other to lift his rifle skyward to avoid shooting his companion.

She blasted the first with force magic, sending him

hurtling back into his partner. They dropped in a tangle, and she ran ahead to finish the battle, only to skid to a stop before reaching them. A canvas bag was bound to a nearby post. A familiar canvas bag. She swore, then said, "I have a satchel charge here."

Ruby quipped, "Did you bring enough for the whole class?" as Idryll somersaulted over the electrical blast her opponent had fired at her. She kicked backward as soon as she landed. The blow caught her foe in mid-turn, slamming him on the hip and knocking him off balance. She turned and slashed with her claws, cutting into the arm he raised in a panicked defense and slashing along the part of his chest it failed to protect. She finished him with a jump kick to the face.

The discovery of explosives had increased the threat significantly, so she was willing to risk potentially killing her opponent to take him out of the fight in a single exchange. She surveyed the space around her and spotted an object that looked out of place. "Is it a boring green fabric bag?"

Morrigan replied, "Yep."

"Got one here too, on the side of a huge metal thing that looks like it's storage for electricity, or a meter, or transformer, or something. I don't know equipment."

Ruby instructed, "Work faster. Look for hostages, security guards, anyone we need to evacuate. D, the clock is ticking. Call Andrews and let him know about the bombs. Call Alejo, too. Call whoever you can think of. Also, make getting the cameras up a priority. We have to find out if there are civilians here to rescue."

He replied, "On it."

Idryll ran at top speed, counting on frequent turns and cuts to keep her from getting blasted by anyone above. She rounded a corner, and a Drow swung a thick club at her head, forcing her to slide. She came up on the other side and spun in time to stop the next effort to bash her an inch away from her eyes. The tiger-woman snapped out a kick, but he raised a leg to block it and countered with a shuffle to slam his body into hers.

Idryll met his charge and accepted the impact, her increased strength more than a match for his. She pistoned an elbow out at his head, but he blocked it with one hand and punched at her with the other. She didn't see the dagger, only discovered its presence as it jabbed into her side. Fortunately, the blade was shallow, extending only an inch beyond his knuckles. She growled, "Dirty trick," and slammed her fist down onto his forearm, breaking it.

Idryll stabbed the claws on her other hand into his thigh, carefully avoiding major blood vessels but penetrating the muscle. The limb gave out, and she delivered a knee to his head as he went down, with only a fraction of the power she could've put behind it. She dashed toward the next. Instead of engaging, he turned and ran. "Mine's running."

Morrigan replied, "Mine, too."

Ruby said, "Same all around. Clearly, we need to get the hell out of here. I haven't seen anyone else. Maybe only one guard was on duty when they broke in."

Demetrius advised, "Can't get the cameras, sorry. Whoever is running protection for them is good. I made the calls. People are on the way."

Frustration at the potential for leaving innocents in the building filled her, but only one logical option remained. "Okay, follow them out. Try to catch one of the bastards. I think we need to get some inside information on this new version of the Drow's gang."

She raced outside on the heels of a trio of enemies. A glimmer off to the side caught her attention as one of their foes created a portal and stepped through. Ruby cursed and muttered, "Where are those anti-magic backpacks when you need them?" She grabbed a lightning disc and threw it, but one of the three in front of her had turned, and he batted it aside with a burst of force.

A second stopped as well and summoned a wreath of shadow tentacles to grab her. Ruby snarled, "No way, no how," as she drew her sword. The blade whipped through the waving purple strands, severing them, and her battle fury increased as the sentient beings inside the weapon urged her on. She wasn't quite at the point where she could effectively cast through the sword, but it was adequate to intercept other magics. She spun it and grounded out a blast of incoming lightning. Two on one was too much to handle in the chaos, especially if she wanted to capture one before they escaped. She sheathed her sword and distracted them with gunfire over their heads, then hurled another lightning disc at their feet, enveloping them in electricity.

Her display had warned her of the incoming PDA drones, thanks to the locator tags they hadn't yet removed. They swooped in, and she reflexively dodged as one came toward her. Instead of attacking her, it sent a stream of bullets at the pair she was fighting, one of whom managed to summon a magical shield in defense. Ruby snarled, "At least they're not after us for once."

Morrigan replied, "That's a useful change."

Ruby called up her magic to finish the one still standing in front of her. Then everything went topsy-turvy as the building behind them exploded with far more force than she'd imagined possible after hearing about the satchel charges. As she sailed through the air, an errant thought crossed her mind. *Hmm. Maybe batteries are more explosive than I realized.*

She hit the ground hard, despite her magical cocoon, and the world went dark.

CHAPTER THREE

Ruby returned to consciousness and looked around her, deducing from the continued chaos that she'd only been out for a few seconds. People picked themselves up off the ground in all directions, and she tried to do the same. She wobbled for a moment, then forced her tumbling mind to focus on the nearest enemy. He skipped into a portal before she could grab him, and she suppressed the urge to follow him through, given that the Drow had clearly been waiting for them. *That might be exactly what he wants.* She warned her partners, "Don't go through the portals."

Idryll groaned, "Ow. The Hat is going to pay for that."

Morrigan chuckled, but the sound held a note of pain as well. "I think we need to set a trap for this guy. Involving sharks. Hungry ones."

Ruby looked around for stragglers they could still capture, but all the vandals had gotten away on their own or assisted by their comrades. *Except for any who were inside when it blew. Surely Alejo won't blame us for that.* "Yeah, we'll put up a big sign that says 'Anti-human rally here. No cover charge for hat-wearing Drow.' That'll be great."

Demetrius interjected, "Sheriff and PDA inbound."

Morrigan said, "That's our exit cue. Let's get out of here." She opened a portal, and Ruby saw the bunker shimmering and wavering within it.

"I'm going to stay and talk to Alejo. You guys go and be ready to bail me out if things go wrong."

Idryll replied, "After a week or so, maybe. You *are* a criminal, after all, and should have to pay for your misdeeds."

Ruby said, "Shut it. Go." With a wave to a PDA drone circling nearby, she cast a veil and repositioned under cover of her illusory invisibility. She watched from a distance as Sheriff Valentina Alejo's car pulled in, and the officer climbed out and dispatched her team. The sheriff herself stayed by her vehicle, perhaps sensing that Ruby was nearby and might want to talk.

She approached from behind, and once within earshot whispered, "Don't turn around. People will think you're crazy."

Alejo flinched slightly in surprise. "Like that would be a change. You're invisible, I suppose?"

"Yup."

The other woman sighed audibly, pulled out her phone, and made a show of pretending to punch numbers, then raised it to her ear and turned toward where Ruby's voice had come from. "Know anything about this that we don't?"

Ruby shrugged, even though she knew she was invisible. *Habit is a powerful thing.* "It was the Drow. The same one that's been causing trouble all along."

The sheriff nodded. "Thanks for the earlier tip-off about him. We've done a little research on whether other cities are experiencing this sort of thing. You know, in case it's a systematic effort to destabilize the country or something."

Ruby blinked. *Damn, that's thinking big. That possibility never even occurred to me.* "Is it?"

It was Alejo's turn to shrug. "Not that we can find. We've concluded it's not a Drow thing. It's a scumbag thing."

She gave a short laugh. "Well, that part is damn accurate, anyway. I guess I don't have any other useful information, other than that someone saw our boy in the Darkest Night casino, so there may be a connection with other Drow in our city."

Alejo asked, "And the Council?"

She sighed. "Couldn't say. That Elnyier person is kind of an enigma."

"Must be a canny politician, though, to have taken the leadership away from the other guy."

She's not wrong about that. "That's a strong assessment, as I understand it. Hungry for power and authority. Maybe not as interested in the responsibilities that come along with it."

Alejo changed the subject. "Also, as far as we know, our gang leader doesn't have his fingers in the Aces mess, either."

Ruby frowned. "I heard about the building blowing up, but it never occurred to me that it could be the Drow. I guess because they're not anti-human at all."

The other woman nodded. "Agreed, but we check

everything as a matter of procedure. Obviously, there's not too much evidence available given the big boom, but everyone I've talked to is of the opinion Worldspan caused that particular event."

Ruby sighed because that still didn't make sense to her. "What the hell are they doing? What's to gain by fighting with other security companies?" She'd discussed that question at length with her father, and they'd concluded it couldn't be *only* about business. Someone or something else had to be involved. A personal grudge, maybe.

Alejo paused to grab her walkie-talkie and answer a question, then replied, "Agreed. It's weird. We weren't able to interview the principals of Aces, and Worldspan isn't returning our calls, either."

"The Aces people didn't want to talk?"

"The dwarf is in the wind. No one's seen him since the event. The human is in the hospital, and we haven't received clearance from the doctors to talk to him yet."

She remembered hearing generally good things about Grentham's partner. "Is he bad?"

Alejo nodded. "Apparently, he died at the scene but had some snazzy tech that brought him back and stabilized him until they could get help. Despite what the movies suggest, it takes a while to recover from something like that. Pretty hard on the body."

"So, what you're saying is, we'll be seeing him on one of those daytime talk shows discussing what lies on the other side?"

Alejo laughed, the inappropriate and poorly timed joke breaking through her defenses. "Yes, exactly."

Demetrius whispered in her ear, "You're about to have company. PDA."

Ruby said, "The Paranormal Defense Agency is about to crash this party."

Alejo nodded. "Smart choice to call them, too. For all the good it did."

They talked a little more about the situation between Worldspan and Aces but managed no additional connections or conclusions. As Paul Andrews approached, Alejo repositioned herself to create a triangle with each of them at a point. The PDA director frowned at her motion. Then understanding blossomed on his face. He said, "Sheriff. Masked marauder. Which one are you?"

Ruby laughed. "Your favorite, *Paulie*."

He stared at the ground and shook his head with a sigh. "Awesome." Then he lifted his chin and looked in her general direction, misjudging her location by about a foot. "Thanks for the call. Too bad it was too late."

She replied, "Unfortunately, we didn't find out about the break-in until they'd been here for a while, to judge from the way they had the place wired up. Bastards."

Andrews turned to Alejo and asked, "Any leads on why they attacked this place?"

"Nothing yet."

Ruby offered, "The company that co-owns it with the casino families has been spreading money around to anti-magical causes."

Alejo let out a soft groan, and Andrews said, "Yeah, that'll do it. Such a *smart* thing to do if you're operating in a place called Magic City. People are idiots."

She laughed. Those words, and the tone he'd used to

deliver them, could have come right out of her mouth. "So, the upshot of this is that the company loses some money, and the casinos will have to shift to a new power supplier for a while. I doubt we can chalk this up to inter-company warfare."

Andrews shrugged. "I can't imagine a power company acting that way, but then before I came here, I wouldn't have said that private security companies were likely to go to war with one another, either."

Alejo replied, "True that."

Ruby said, "So you think that's what's going on there? They're simply fighting for territory?"

Andrews replied, "I've given that question some deep thought and talked it over with my team. That explanation doesn't sit right with me. The expense versus profit ratio is way off, especially on the Aces side. I mean, Worldspan is big and could potentially float the cost of such operations from other cash sources, counting on later contracts to make it up. But Aces? No, I don't see it. They must've felt threatened, more than just economically."

Ruby asked, "Which means what?"

He lifted empty palms on spread arms. "Your guess is as good as mine. The only result I can see outside of the companies involved is that the fracas sows chaos in the city, which keeps the casino owners off-balance and concerned."

Alejo replied, "Which makes them more likely to depend on their leadership and possibly more willing to consider stepping away from their businesses?"

Ruby offered, "Sounds rational. Maybe I'll ask around, see what I can find out on that topic."

Alejo nodded. "I'll do the same."

Andrews confirmed, "Me, too. Let's funnel all information through the sheriff."

Ruby laughed. "Don't you like me, Agent Andrews?"

He shook his head. "I still think you create more problems than you solve. It's best for us to keep official distance between us regardless, though."

"Guess I won't visit your bedroom again, then." She walked away as Alejo asked, "What the hell is she talking about?" and Andrews responded with a deep sigh.

CHAPTER FOUR

Grentham was a fierce figure stalking through the hallways of Mountainview hospital in Las Vegas. He'd figured the larger facility would be better able to treat serious injuries than the one in Ely, and he visited every six months or so to ensure he had a spot to portal to safely.

He recalled stepping out of the combat zone and into a little-used hallway near the emergency room. Carrying his partner had been difficult even with magically assisted muscles because Jared was tall, and all things considered, poorly balanced. *It's a good thing I didn't have to throw him as a weapon.*

The amusement of the thought failed to reach his face, which was locked in a scowl. Now and again, a hospital worker would glance at him, seeming like they were about to say something, but his expression stilled any comments before they manifested.

Grentham spotted his people flanking a door and knew he'd found his destination. He exchanged greetings with the pair, a dwarf and an elf who'd been part of his crew since the earliest days, and asked for a status update. They confirmed that there had been no excitement, which was exactly what he wanted to hear. The wench from Worldspan might still try to finish the job. He wouldn't lessen his vigilance until she was six feet beneath the ground.

His partner's new temporary home was smaller than most hospital rooms Grentham had been in. He'd insisted on a single for security purposes, and the chamber held almost no empty space. His partner was lying back in bed with the upper portion of the mattress raised at a slight angle.

Jared managed a smile despite the discomfort his wound was causing him. Bandages covered more of him than Grentham would've expected, given the injury. The wounded man's voice was a little croakier than normal. "Welcome to the most boring place on the planet. On either planet. Any planet."

Grentham laughed and turned to the room's third occupant, an elf sitting in an industrial-looking recliner, glaring moderately over the top of a magazine. "Haven't you been entertaining him like I asked?"

His subordinate rolled his eyes. "Sure. A little song, a little dance, some juggling. He was a distinctly unappreciative audience." The dry sarcasm made both patient and visitor laugh.

Jared shifted with a groan. "So, I would've thought you'd be too busy packing to visit."

Grentham shook his head. "Gotta have priorities, and checking on my partner ranks higher than running for the hills, at least at the current moment. What do the doctors say?"

His partner shrugged, which caused the IV line in his arm to twitch. He adjusted it with a move that looked like he'd done it a hundred times already that day and had the same number of fixes left before sleeping. "Well, the whole dying thing was pretty hard on my body. Who knew, right?"

He managed a dark, coughing laugh. "But I should make a full recovery before too long." His voice dropped as if sharing a secret. "I convinced them they needed to do everything they could to get me out of here since it might be dangerous for me to stay."

Grentham chuckled. "So, what, they gave you some magical miracle drugs they would've kept secret if you hadn't warned them? I think you might overestimate your persuasive abilities." He moved to the low shelf that ran along the wall and hopped up on it to sit. The world outside the window showed nothing particularly interesting, some mountains on the horizon, but fortunately also didn't appear to offer an opportunity for snipers to shoot into the room. "Pretty view."

"I'd rather be in the office, although technically I guess the office is rubble at the moment. Speaking of which, what's next for Aces?"

Grentham couldn't keep some of the sadness he felt from showing on his face as a frown. "No one new is going to hire us for a while since we're short on people and supplies, not to mention getting our asses kicked in a way that doesn't breed confidence in potential clients. So, until we can properly rebuild, we have the opportunity to focus on payback."

Jared nodded. "I hoped you'd say that. Sell the diamonds, use them to fund it."

"You put them in your safe deposit box, remember? I can't exactly go in and pretend to be you. Banks are pretty good at magical detection stuff, not to mention there's almost certainly an anti-magic emitter in the vault."

His partner sighed. "Well, I'll have to get out of this bed and retrieve them." He made motions as if he would, then fell back, making a noise somewhere between a laugh and a moan. "Yeah, maybe another day or two."

Grentham shook his head. "Maybe four or five, by the looks of you. You shouldn't push it. This is a good moment for a healing rest in a secure spot hidden away from the troubles of Magic City. Anyway, I have plenty of cash available to handle this particular project. You can pay me back your half later."

"Start with Smith, and we'll make it a sixty-forty split to your advantage."

"Done. It'll be my distinct pleasure. What are your thoughts on how to do it?"

Jared replied, "I've had a lot of time to consider that question, lying here not being entertained by your nanny." The elf gave him a dirty look, but it held no malice. "My first idea was to set up a meet and ambush them, but they'd have to expect something like that. I mean, they can't think for a moment that we're unaware they put Worldspan up to this."

Grentham nodded. "Agreed."

"So, you're going to have to stalk them. Like a hunter."

He laughed. "You have your magicals confused. That's the Kilomea way."

Jared shrugged. "I don't have access to a Kilomea. I have a dwarf. But the principles are the same. You can't go in guns blazing. They have bigger guns and more of them."

A thought occurred to him, and he tumbled it around in his mind for a few seconds to decide how bad an idea it was. Then, he decided he didn't care and shared it. "I think we should see if Scimitar has any decency left in her."

Jared shook his head slowly, more like he was thinking than rejecting the notion outright. "Lot of risk in that option. If she decides to tell Sloane, it could turn into a perfect double-cross ambush."

Grentham nodded. "I get that, believe me. I don't want to walk into a trap, and I'll be careful no matter how we do it. But I sensed some reluctance in her during our last conversation. Did I imagine that?"

"No, I thought she seemed that way, too. Still, it could have been simply good business practice, softening the blow. Not burning her bridges."

He raised an eyebrow. "You think she cares about that sort of thing?"

Jared laughed, then grabbed his side as if it had hurt him to do so. "Good point. She's not exactly overly concerned with interpersonal niceties."

"Very well said, and agreed."

He shrugged. "It's your head, partner, so it's your call."

Grentham jumped down from the ledge and looked his friend in the eye. "Actually, it'll be your head, too. If I open this particular can of worms, Scimitar or not, they'll be irked enough to come after both of us. Hard."

"So, what else is new? They've been coming after us all along. Your people have security well in hand here, so my safety isn't a huge deal. If you think talking to the infomancer is the way to go, I say go ahead and do it. Although, if hiring a Kilomea is still on the table, that might work, too."

Grentham shook his head. "Can't outsource something this personal." He punched Jared lightly on the shoulder. "Don't worry, partner. I've got this."

CHAPTER FIVE

Ruby was buried under the covers with a pillow over her head when a discreet knock sounded on the door. A voice from beyond said, "Miss Ruby?"

She called back, "Ruby is dead. No one here but us cats." Idryll, in her domestic disguise on the pillow beside her, swatted playfully at her head.

Matthias's precise tones replied, "That's unfortunate, as a messenger has arrived, requesting her presence at a certain shop in the kemana that she's visited before."

That piece of news got her moving. She threw off the covers and said, "Tell her I'll be there within a half-hour." She sped for the shower to knock some semblance of intelligence back into her brain.

Idryll accompanied her on the quick walk through the kemana. Ruby had decided against portaling straight there, needing the time to get her thoughts in order. It would be difficult to take on another task, even for the Drow who'd been so much help to her.

Ruby thought of the blades that rode in her boots,

which had saved her life on more than one occasion, and gave a soft sigh. *A debt owed is a debt owed, and one can't always control when the bill comes due.*

She opened the shop door and entered without breaking stride, then stopped at the unexpected sight of not one but two Dark Elves awaiting her. Shentia smiled and offered a nod of greeting. Nylotte gave her that *look*, the one that combined obvious disappointment with a sort of hopelessness that the other person could ever rise above their limitations.

Diana had confided that the woman's attitude was mostly an act but made her promise to go along with the game. Ruby nodded at both in turn. "Greetings."

Shentia rose from her antique chair and gestured toward a door Ruby had never been through. "Follow me." It opened onto a staircase, which provided access to the shop's top floor. Ruby hadn't put together that the upper level was there, despite having seen the second story from outside. The stairs led to a quaint living room, with a small kitchen to one side and a closed door on the other. Nylotte took the wingback chair in the middle of the U-shaped arrangement of furniture, and Idryll and Ruby chose the loveseat, leaving the couch for their host.

Shentia appeared after a minute with a silver serving tray, on which rested teacups, a pot, and an array of cookies. She set it on the table in the center of the seats, then perched on the edge of the couch. "Have some."

Idryll's hand snaked out and snatched at the nearest, causing them all to laugh. Through a mouthful of crumbs, Idryll said, "What? They're cookies, and I'm hungry."

Their host smiled. "That's what they're for. It's always

lovely to see someone fully enjoy themselves." Nylotte drummed her fingers on the arm of the chair, and Shentia seemed to take it as a sign. She said, "I'm sure you're wondering why I asked you here."

Ruby nodded. "I figured you needed me to do something for you, but I would say Nylotte's presence here seems to argue against that."

Diana's mentor laughed darkly. "Well, it does most likely involve doing something. But for both of us, rather than just Shentia."

The snarky part of Ruby's mind observed, *probably means we won't get any credit toward our debt*. The rest of her brain followed her body, which turned slightly in Shentia's direction as the other woman spoke. "Events in Ely have us concerned, as members of the Drow community here on Earth. We have each worked long and hard to create a space for ourselves where we have no reason to fear humans and live cooperatively with other magicals. This is a continuing challenge, of course, based on how people often view the Drow."

Nylotte grumbled, "Not always incorrectly, which is the particular problem we face here."

Shentia nodded. "Indeed. Elnyier is not representing our people well as the head of the Council."

Ruby sighed. "I have to admit that's my opinion too, although I would say she's not representing *anyone* well. Quite a disappointment, really. What's your beef with her?"

Shentia sipped her tea and nibbled the edge of a cookie before responding. "We agree that were we in her place; we would have already dealt harshly with the one behind the anti-human movement. His actions aren't good for our people, not good for magicals in general, and obviously quite bad for the humans he targets. Her responsibility to address it is twofold, both as leader of the Council and representative of the Drow in this kemana. She has failed in this task, and the scope of her failure grows with each new attack."

Nylotte interjected, "Thus, someone must remove her from power."

Ruby's brain went momentarily offline. Then she shook her head to clear the fog and asked, "You mean you want me to kill her?"

The other woman chuckled darkly. "Well, that would be both efficient and effective. You could opt for less militant options first, of course. Perhaps she could be removed by vote, as she arranged matters against Lord Maldren?"

Ruby nodded thoughtfully. "Maybe. I know at least one member of the Council who might throw his support to another candidate, so that gives our contingent two votes at a minimum. It might be possible to convince enough others to join in to defeat her. I can definitely give that a try."

Shentia scowled. "Of course, the other issue is the Drow male who is behind all this chaos."

Idryll interrupted, "Ruby calls him the Hat."

Both Dark Elves stared at her, and Ruby felt silly. *Oh, there's going to be payback for that one, kitty cat.* She explained, "He tends to wear a hat when he's out in public. It's a simple way to spot him, especially with drones and cameras."

Shentia replied, "Because he wants others to notice him.

That's not a surprise. He requires publicity for his actions to have meaning."

Ruby asked, "Why the sudden interest? I mean, no offense, but he's been in town causing trouble for a while."

Nylotte shrugged. "Multiple reasons. First, when his group was a mixture of magicals, that was one thing. Others could have perceived it as a grassroots effort, diverse beings with shared interests coming together. Now that he's fielding mainly Drow, it's easy to judge his actions as something more sinister, even though they are no different than before. We have enough bad press as it is."

"That makes sense. Can't *you* do anything about him?"

Shentia lifted an eyebrow and a hint of a grin formed on her lips. "We are. We're sending you."

Nylotte shook her head with a small smile at her companion's comment. "Politically, we can't act while Elnyier is in power. It's her responsibility, and it would be inappropriate for us to undermine her by taking it on."

So, ghosting her is fine, but helping her isn't. It's a good thing the position of Mirra doesn't require elections or politicking. I'd be so the wrong person for the job if it did. "What about our mutual friends?" *Surely Diana and her people could take out the Drow easily.*

"They're spread thin already, with challenges that affect more people than the events in Ely do. They lack the capacity to add another task. We're on our own, here."

By which you mean I'm on my own here while you pull on the puppet strings. Well, my team and I. "Fair enough. What if removing her from Council leadership doesn't work?"

Nylotte shrugged. "Then we'll have to consider our

options. All in all, getting her voted out would be best for everyone involved."

Especially for Elnyier, given the alternative. "Any ideas on how to deal with the Hat and his gang?"

Shentia replied, "Once Elnyier can no longer use her leadership role to block the effort, it should be simple enough to rally the rest of the Council to bring the wills of those they lead to bear on that issue. If the entire community rises against him, he'll have to stop, either because he recognizes he no longer has support or because the larger group takes action against him. Either way, the problem is solved."

Idryll looked at Nylotte and said, "Apologies for the personal question. I get why Shentia is concerned. She lives here. Why do you care?"

"It is a rude inquiry, but the answer is simple, and I'm willing to share it. Inappropriately, others often judge me by the actions of other Drow. Thus, when one of us acts badly, it stains me. In fact, it stains all of us."

Ruby replied, "We'll do our best to take care of this for you. Let's hope we can do it the easy way." *Because having to kill Elnyier over politics doesn't seem right. If it comes to that, I'll have to find a better option.*

CHAPTER SIX

Ruby's vantage point showed an array of people, some of them clearly looking for trouble. She tensed, ready to intervene, as a pair of dwarves bumped into a trio of college kids. Fortunately, the situation resolved itself with only a few jokes and a gruff apology exchanged. She shook her head. "Mick, I'll take a refill."

The bartender nodded and pulled her another drink. Morrigan's voice came over the comm. "Bored?"

Ruby shielded her mouth with her hand and replied, "It's not the best night I've ever spent at the Grinding Axes, that's for sure."

Idryll said, "Think of it this way. At least you're not outside on the rooftops where your natural clumsiness would put your life at risk."

She sighed and accepted the drink that the dwarven bartender handed over to her. It was one of the abbey's special brews and featured an unusual taste she couldn't quite identify. Some sort of greenish spice. *Not rosemary, but something in that family, maybe. I'll need to ask Abbott*

Thomas for another tasting. Every so often, the head of the abbey put together a small meal and talk about the beers they were brewing, debuting new varieties to a trusted inner circle she was unexpectedly and most gratefully a part of.

Demetrius said, "You just miss me, I'm sure. It's natural to pine after someone as awesome as I am. Not something to be ashamed of."

Idryll and Morrigan made kissing noises over the comm, their latest way to poke fun at her relationship with the infomancer. She replied in a flat tone, "Truer words were never spoken. Does anyone see him yet?" A chorus of negatives came over the comms. "Anything useful on the drones?"

"Not on mine, and since we lost the video feeds from the PDA, I have nothing else to offer."

Morrigan replied, "Oh, I think you have *plenty* to offer. Are you sure you don't want to dump her and date me instead?"

Ruby's follow-up would have been appropriately crude, but an elf slid onto the stool next to her, disrupting her concentration. His voice was lower than she would have expected at first glance. "Hey."

She gave him a fast visual review. Tall, thin, with long, perfectly brushed golden hair. Earrings, not too ostentatious, and a lip ring she kind of liked. But his eyes were disquieting, something superior in them that set off alarm bells. *Not a threat, but not my type, either.* She replied neutrally, "Hi."

"I think I've seen you in here before, usually with a group, is that right?"

Morrigan whispered, "D, are you getting this? He's hitting on your girlfriend."

Ruby restrained laughter at her sister's comment. "Yeah, once or twice at least."

He said something in response, but she lost it as the opening door snatched her attention. She interrupted him. "I'm sorry. I've been waiting for someone, and they just got here. Nice chatting with you." She slipped off her chair and exchanged a couple of words with the other bartender, Domick's twin, Jastrum. Her brain shifted into battle mode as she headed over to the table where her target sat alone.

The dwarf and elf who'd entered with him weren't with him, which was notable. *Protection, then, not company. Interesting.* She whispered, "I've got him. Get close in case we need to follow him."

Ruby covered the rest of the distance, took the seat across from him, and nodded a greeting.

He scowled but returned the nod. "No gift drink this time?"

She shrugged. "I thought you might not trust it. It seems as if you're a little nervous." She tilted her head toward one of the guards that had entered with him.

He laughed. "Could be that I am. Good instincts on your part."

"I'll buy you one though."

He replied, "Won't say no to that. Be right back." Grentham walked up to the bar, and when Jas looked over at her, she nodded. He returned several moments later with a tall glass of beer in his hand. As he moved into the seat with a groan, he asked, "So, what do you want this time?"

She put on an affronted expression. "What makes you think I want something?"

He took a deep drink and replied, "Please. Everyone wants something."

Sad but true. "Okay, you've got me figured out. I'll tell you what I want. Then you can do the same, how's that?"

"Free country."

His clipped tone brought out the same in her. "Elnyier's a menace. She has to go."

He managed to swallow before breaking out in laughter, loud enough that a couple of people looked over to see what was going on. "Well, that's rather bold and direct. Not that you're wrong. What did she do to tick you off?"

Ruby sipped at her drink. "Long story, and boring. Short version is that some folks I owe want her gone, so it's my job to get her gone."

He stared at her through lowered brows. "Gone, gone?"

"Only if there's no other way. I *really* need to find another way, since I don't have the contacts to manage the other thing, regardless. Figured maybe we could vote her off."

He pulled on his beard thoughtfully. "Could work, with the right amount of persuasion, extortion, and manipulation."

She laughed. "I'm okay at persuasion, inexperienced at extortion but willing to learn, and dead useless at manipulation. Definitely going to need some help." She finished her beer and signaled for another round for them both. "So, what is it you want, aside from a free drink?"

His brows lowered, and his face wrinkled in anger. "For bloody Worldspan Security to fall back into the deep cesspool they crawled out of. Preferably screaming all the way down."

Ruby nodded, trying to convey sympathy without showing any pity. *He wouldn't respond well to that.* "I heard your building blew up. Figured it might have something to do with them, given their similar experience in the not-too-distant past."

His eyes followed his finger as he drew patterns in the condensation his glass had left on the table. "They suck. A lot. Like, *a lot* a lot."

"What's the deal with you two? Where's the profit in physically going after each other?"

He met her gaze again. "It's not about profit. They attacked us for some different reason."

She noticed he didn't reference the fact that Aces had started it or that they might've had an ulterior motive as well. "Why do you think they did it?"

He lowered his voice to a hint above a whisper. "It's Sloane's wife. She hired us after he died to handle things for her in the city, then apparently decided she liked Worldspan better."

His words didn't quite ring true to her ears, but she wasn't interested in plumbing the depths of his veracity. "Will you help with the Council?"

He spent a minute drinking in silence, clearly turning over the question in his mind. Finally, he replied, "On one condition. If Sloane attacks me and mine again, you bring whatever Mist Elves you can rally in support."

She nodded. "I'll try."

He chuckled, but it held no humor. "I suppose that's all I

can ask for at this point. I presume you want to put forth your father for leader of the Council?"

"Do you have a better idea?"

"No. But you should make sure he knows it could get nasty. I'd start taking precautions now."

Rayar Achera asked, "When are Council politics *not* nasty?" He was staring into the fire with his back toward her. His study was warm and the drink in her hand a perfect cellar temperature.

Ruby had shared the details of her conversations with the Drow women and with Grentham. Her father hadn't appeared overly surprised by any of it. She said, "You all seemed pretty amicable to me."

He turned to her and shook his head. "Illusion, more or less. When there isn't a power vacuum or serious imbalance, we mostly get along fine. When there is, the knives come out and everyone's seeking an advantage."

"Now that your numbers are smaller, the likelihood of power shifts is greater."

He nodded. "It takes convincing fewer people, which probably means less compromise to accomplish things. I don't suppose this can wait until we replace our lost members?"

Ruby shook her head. "They seemed quite serious that it should happen quickly. Besides, every day she's in charge is another day that the Drow and his gang are causing trouble for humans and magicals alike."

"Fair." He tipped the last of the whiskey in his tumbler

down his throat, then set the glass down with a sigh. "Of course, I'll do it. You're right. The time for action is now if we want to keep things from spiraling out of control even further. I'll need your help to convince people to throw their support behind me."

"I'll do what I can."

"Hopefully, the two of us together can get it done. Guess we might as well get started."

She frowned. "Right now? It's nearly midnight."

He laughed and looked almost eager for what lay ahead. "Politics never sleeps, daughter. Welcome to my battlefield."

CHAPTER SEVEN

Ruby led the way through the Darkest Night casino's entrance, and as always was immediately entranced by the nighttime sky that seemed to extend to infinity overhead. Demetrius gave her a gentle push to keep her moving, and Daphne and Liam laughed as they joined her. The dwarf said, "How many times have you been in casinos? You know it's all smoke and mirrors."

Ruby shook her head. "That doesn't lessen its beauty one bit." She was in her human disguise. Of the present company, only Demetrius had seen her without it. Her apparent non-magical status earned her some glares from the magicals around, not only limited to the Dark Elves. She muttered, "Feels more hostile than usual."

Daphne replied, "My friends at the Ebon Dragon see the same thing. We're not putting our best foot forward at the moment, community-wise."

Liam grunted. "None of that nonsense happens at the Underground. Anyone acts like a jerk, and we throw him out straight away."

Demetrius laughed. "You all are always looking for a reason to throw people. That's just a convenient excuse."

The dwarf grinned. "You're not wrong. Unlike in most casinos, security is the most sought-after job in ours."

Ruby checked her watch and warned, "If we don't get moving, we'll miss our reservation time."

Daphne poked her in the arm. "You're the one who's stargazing, sweetheart."

Liam poked Daphne. "Hey. I'm the only one you should call sweetheart."

Ruby and Demetrius exchanged smiles as the group headed for the restaurant, simply called Dusk. She had chosen their destination for the evening, both because she wanted to try out the new menu and because she was hoping to do a little reconnaissance and get a sense of what things were like on the ground in the Dark Elf casino. Once they were in their seats, after the drink orders and before the arrival of the waiter to take their food requests, Ruby said, "I have a confession to make." She released her illusion, letting the others see her in her natural Mist Elf form.

Liam's jaw dropped open. "Well. That's something."

Daphne's mouth formed a perfect O, then she enthused, "That explains *so much*. I always thought it was weird that a human was going into technomancy, although your explanation was plausible enough to deflect my suspicions."

Ruby chuckled. "I'm sorry I had to deceive you. It's a long story involving a prophecy and my parents protecting me. It turns out the prophecy was true, and now that I've become the *Mirra* of the Mist Elves, I can quit pretending."

Liam looked at Demetrius and asked, "You knew?"

He shrugged. "Not at first, but eventually. It wasn't my secret to share. Besides, the danger sounded pretty real."

Daphne cocked her head. "Why?"

Ruby replied, "The *Mirra* is the leader of the Mist Elves. Basically, I speak for all of us."

Liam whistled. "Damn. No pressure, right? Do you get a crown and a palace?"

She laughed. "Sort of. The castle *is* pretty nice, though." She chose not to mention the crown that had magically melted into her head to record her personality for future *Mirra* to access.

Their waiter, a young Dark Elf male, arrived and took their orders for appetizers and meals. When he left, another person approached the table. Ruby nodded. "Elnyier."

The Drow casino owner and current leader of the Council nodded in return, gazing down at the four of them. "*Mirra* Ruby Achera. Are you going to introduce me to your friends?"

Ruby complied, and they exchanged pleasantries on both sides. She said, "Your casino is gorgeous."

The other woman smiled, but the pleasantness didn't reach her eyes. "Thank you very much. We think it's the most beautiful one on the Strip, of course." The smile faded to neutrality. "I hope you enjoy your meal. I gave instructions to the kitchen to make your experience extra special. Best regards to your father."

She turned and walked away, and Demetrius whispered, "Does that mean she's poisoned us?"

Ruby fought to keep a neutral expression on her face, suppressing the scowl that wanted to rise. *Can't let her see that she got to me.* "I don't imagine she would do something so obvious, especially after people saw her interacting with us in public." She watched from the corner of her eye as Elnyier sat at a table on the edge of the dining room. She was joined a minute later by another Dark Elf. Ruby blocked her mouth with her hand and whispered to her boyfriend, "No hat, but I think that could be him."

Demetrius replied, "That's not good."

Liam asked, "What are you two on about?"

Ruby shook her head. "That woman is the leader of the Council, in addition to being the owner, or at least one of the owners of this casino. I think she's meeting with someone involved in the anti-human movement."

Daphne said, "Not exactly the sort of relationship you want to see a Council member encouraging, I imagine."

Ruby replied, "Indeed."

The witch said, "They look like they're on a date."

Demetrius said, "Maybe they are."

"What?"

Her boyfriend shrugged. "Evil people need love too."

While the others had been bantering, Ruby had been keeping an eye on the other woman. She sighed. "I was hoping the people around her would dislike her, proving she was some sort of tyrant. But she seems to have their support, at least the ones in here." She paused as a pair of humans entered the room, walked over to Elnyier's table, and shook hands with her. "Dang. Apparently, folks from outside Magic City find her appealing, too. Those two are on the state gaming commission. When I've seen them at Spirits, they've been much more frowny."

The arrival of their meals forestalled discussion. Instead of what they'd ordered, the waiter delivered a tray full of family-style tasting dishes. He grinned and explained, "Some of everything on the menu. Whatever you particularly like, I'll happily get you more of. Anything you need, just ask." They tucked into the meal, and despite her distaste for the woman herself, Ruby had to admit that the Dark Elf's restaurant was fantastic.

All the more reason to get that craft beer restaurant online in Spirits, give this place some competition. The conversation stayed light until they'd finished dessert and waddled toward the door to walk off some of the calories on the Strip. She took a parting look at Elnyier and shook her head. Once they were outside, and arguably beyond the range of any microphones that might be listening in from Darkest Night, Ruby said, "We need to figure out what the hell her game is. I thought it was a power grab on the Council, but now I'm not so sure."

Demetrius replied, "Assuming she uses transport other than portal, I can follow her with a drone. Keep a few around the casino at all times; pick her up when she comes out."

Ruby nodded. "I can't imagine she'll give us anything, but you have the small ones that shouldn't spook her, so you might as well. Keep an eye out for her boyfriend, too."

He grinned. "Well, at least you're one up on her there."

"Huh?"

"Boyfriends. Hers is a marauding jerk. Yours is a brilliant and handsome infomancer. Much better."

Ruby laughed and grabbed his hand, interlacing her fingers with his. "So very true and humble, as usual. Now, how about we all head down to Spirits and grab an after-dinner drink?" *And let my dad know Elnyier's up to something with the gaming commission. He's not going to be any more pleased with that information than I am.*

CHAPTER EIGHT

Grentham had checked his desks in most of the pawnshops he owned before finally finding the card he was looking for in the next to last. It was one of his Aces business cards, but with a number scrawled on the back. He muttered, "Hope she's still using this," and headed for a public Internet terminal on the Strip.

He entered the cylindrical booth, pulled the door closed, and used a software phone to call the number. It rang ten times before finally connecting. A synthesized voice said, "Hello, Grentham."

He replied, "Scimitar. You owe me."

After a pause, the infomancer said neutrally, "It could be that I do. Perhaps not, though. What do you want?"

"A time and a place to intercept Smith."

"Wait one."

He drummed his fingers on the plastic cocoon that kept his communication private. It wasn't air-conditioned, which encouraged the user to wrap up their business quickly in the Nevada heat. She came back on the line with a chuckle that he found instantly annoying. "Apparently, the fates are aligning for you."

He scowled. "In a good way, for a change?"

She replied, "Could be. They're en route to Magic City. They have an appointment with the real estate agent in an hour or so at this address."

A grin spread across his face as he memorized the information. "Thanks. This doesn't make us even, but it's a step in the right direction."

"That's a matter of opinion, but I sense you don't have time for that discussion at the moment. Not if you're going to make that appointment."

"Until we chat again, then." The line disconnected, and he dropped a portal at his feet, falling through it to the warehouse that was now the secret headquarters of his security company.

The guards had their guns drawn within a few seconds of his arrival, and he nodded in approval. "Good reflexes. It's only me, though. Back to what you were doing."

He and Jared had agreed that keeping their core staff close was essential. They were paying a bonus to those willing to live at the base and leave only by portal to handle their gigs at the casinos that hadn't abandoned them. *Gotta keep whatever cash flowing we can for our people and us.* He'd already had to tap his first-level reserves to cover payroll, and while he had many fallback options remaining, it offended him to have to use any of them.

The rolling crate that served as his locker was right where he'd left it, and he tapped all the locks with his index finger to release them. He strapped on the belt that held the sheathes for his axes, then slipped the weapons into the holders. He hadn't sharpened them lately but trusted they would be adequate for his needs, as always. *The smartest plan would be to throw them from under a veil. Plant one in Smith's skull and the other in his partner's. But what fun would that be?*

He slid into his bulletproof vest and added ballistic thigh pads. He considered taking the shotgun, as its slugs would open almost any door and be equally useful in eliminating his enemies, but decided against it. If his magic and axes couldn't handle it, the big weapon wasn't going to help. Besides, it was bulky for someone his size, and he didn't need anything to slow him unnecessarily.

He grabbed his traveling toolkit, with its lock pick and other clever implements, and made sure his healing flasks were where they belonged. Finally, he donned a shield necklace and mentally reviewed the command word a few times. His magic plus attacking by surprise would give him all the advantage he needed.

Grentham portaled to a spot a block away from his target location. Illusion changed him from a short, stocky armored dwarf into a willowy-tall elf in a business suit, and he headed toward his destination with a spring in his step. The front door was locked, as expected, and more illusion covered the work of the electronic pick. A moment later, he entered the building.

The bottom floor of the four-story structure was supposed to be commercial space, already subdivided into several small shop areas. He found a staircase and climbed to the second level, a huge empty rectangle without interior walls or finishings. Construction tools lay scattered underfoot. The third floor was identical. *Which means they must be up on four unless the appointment information was wrong.*

He ascended the stairs to the top level with an excess of caution, both to avoid being heard and to detect any potential ambush that might lie in wait, should Scimitar prove unreliable. He opened the door as quietly as possible, and voices carried to him through the crack. The first was female, one he remembered mocking him at their last meeting. The wench asked, "Could this floor be an apartment?"

Grentham closed the door silently behind him and approached under a veil. The real estate agent and Thompson stood together on one side of the room, and Smith was by himself, staring out the floor-to-ceiling windows that made up one of the walls. The woman he didn't know replied, "Well, the space is zoned commercial, so that's a bit of a challenge. If the top level is built out as a rental and rented by a company, perhaps for one of its executives, that would probably please both the zoning board and the IRS."

Smith chuckled. "Shell corporation, then. No problem."

From under his veil, Grentham announced, "Oh, there's definitely a problem, believe me."

He released the magical invisibility and simultaneously created a portal behind Thompson and the real estate agent. A force blast sent them both tumbling through it, spilling them out into the middle of a Nevada desert, and he closed the portal after them.

Smith was competent. He'd always given the man respect for that quality, and his foe had his pistol out almost instantly. Three bullets struck Grentham in the chest, and the vest hidden under his outer shirt absorbed the impacts with ease. He levitated a heavy toolbox in front of him in time to intercept the next barrage of rounds aimed at his head, then sent a fireball spiraling toward his opponent.

Smith tossed a canister between them, and the flaming sphere winked out as if it was never there. Grentham felt his magic vanish and scowled. *Maybe I should've brought the shotgun. When did they start making anti-magic emitters that portable?* While his brain wondered about the reversal, his hands worked by instinct. He drew his axes, gripping one in his right and sending the other tumbling end over end at his opponent.

It struck the arm holding the gun, unfortunately with the handle rather than the blade, but with enough force that his opponent's pistol fell to the floor. Grentham rushed him, ready to plant the ax head deep into his chest, but his foe was fast enough to pull out a baton, flick it to full extension, and block the strike before it could land.

Smith growled, "This has been coming for a long time, you bastard." The other man snapped out a kick that Grentham took on an armored thigh.

He countered with a back fist to the man's chest, meeting a ceramic protective plate that had been invisible behind a perfectly tailored shirt. He gritted his teeth against the pain and whipped the ax around again. They traded a series of blows, baton versus ax, neither of them gaining more than a moment's advantage. His hatred for the other man was almost blinding, which in retrospect was the only explanation for how he'd missed the way his foe was maneuvering the fight's location.

When Smith drove away and came up with Grentham's thrown ax in one hand and the baton in the other, the dwarf shook his head. "Have I ever mentioned how much I hate you? Jared does too, for what it's worth. Even more than I do."

Smith grinned, and it was an ugly sight. "Well, when I finish with you, I'll be sure to pay my respects. A little bird told me he died once. Maybe he'd like to repeat the experience."

Grentham stepped in and chopped down with his ax, but the other man blocked it with its twin and snapped the baton into his ribs. Fortunately, the vest took most of the blow, but what got through still hurt. Two weapons against one, with no magic on to rely upon, turned the fight against him. He managed to pick off the most dangerous blows, taking shots from the baton while avoiding any from the ax.

Had it been axes only, he would've been able to take the other man easily. But his foe's longer reach, combined with the damned baton's extension, meant that any attack he tried earned him a strike before he even got close. The damage was adding up, slowing him down, and finally the weapon caught him on the ankle at the wrong moment, sending him tumbling to the floor.

Smith advanced with an arrogant expression, clearly relishing the moment. Grentham grinned suddenly and said, "So close." His magic had returned an instant before, and he smashed the confused look off Smith's face with a blast of force that sent the man flying through the windows with a huge crash. Grentham limped over to gaze down, nodding in satisfaction at his opponent's broken form on the street four stories below. He muttered, "Before you go into the light, be sure to tell your wench partner and your boss that they're next. Scumbag."

CHAPTER NINE

Julianna Sloane took a moment to brace herself. The last time she'd been in a place like this, it was horrible, literally upending her entire existence. *Well, at least I wasn't in love with this one.*

She nodded, and the medical technician opened the door to the morgue. She set her chin and walked through, stopping beside Vicki Thompson to look down at the body on the table. A sheet covered it, but even so, it wasn't in the proper shape. She asked, "You checked?"

Thompson replied softly, "I did. It's him."

"Does the police story check out?"

Her lieutenant—her *only* lieutenant, now—nodded. "Yeah. He fell from a height, for sure. Too much damage for them to know what happened beforehand. Of course, *we* know the cause. Grentham."

Julianna pressed her lips together to control her anger. "The dead are free. The living still have work to do. Let's take a walk."

The Medical Examiner's office was on the city's

outskirts, but only a dozen blocks or so away from where the incident had occurred. They walked the intervening distance in silence, each woman occupied with her thoughts. When they reached the building where she'd hoped to reside, plywood was visible on the top floor, covering what used to be a window. The pavement before her was ordinary, as if the death of someone she trusted hadn't made an impact on it, or on anything. She shook her head. "I can't possibly live here now."

Thompson replied, "I'm glad to hear that."

With a sigh, Julianna Sloane let her previous plans go. *Again.* It was time for new ones. "Take me to whatever bar is decent and frequented mainly by humans. We need to talk."

Thompson had researched while they waited for their ride, and it was a short trip to the opposite side of the Strip, near the Taka Tower. Julianna inwardly chuckled as they passed the structure, still damaged from the Drow attack upon it. *Apparently, my wanting to live somewhere is the kiss of death. Should probably warn my neighbors in Vegas.* She set the dark thoughts free as Thompson helped her out of the car, and they entered an upscale restaurant.

The bar was chrome and glass, and tuxedoed bartenders moved calmly behind it. The atmosphere was moody and reserved, appropriate for her mental state. She chose a spot in the corner with a curved booth that would hide them from prying eyes. Thompson joined her a moment later, tumblers of whiskey in her hands. Julianna sipped hers, then sighed and set it on the table. "Okay. This is a serious setback, but not a defeat. Until the time we find someone trustworthy enough to elevate, I'm doubling your salary." She'd paid both of her lieutenants exactly the same amount to the penny, so neither would feel she was playing favorites.

Thompson nodded. "Appreciated. I'll review all our personnel files to identify potential candidates."

There wouldn't be any, not soon. Julianna needed to know someone before she could trust them, and she hadn't had time to focus on anyone underneath Smith and Thompson. "We need to get in touch with Worldspan. Whatever their plans are, they have to move faster."

Thompson nodded. "I'll tell them. And when Prash asks for a reason?"

The woman in charge of Worldspan Security was as competent as she was annoying. *Of course, she'll ask, and she'll expect an answer.* "Tell her we require Worldspan to be operating in as many casinos as possible since we don't know where the next opportunity might present itself. However they can get in, they should. Front of house, backstage, personal bodyguards, whatever. What's important is getting inside the casino defenses. Then we'll have the luxury of deciding which target looks most ripe for the taking."

Thompson growled, "Of course, we won't be able to get into The Underground."

Julianna nodded. "I know. The dwarves will stick with Aces, even though they've proven themselves to be a dismal failure. It's too bad we couldn't have killed Grentham instead of Jared."

Her lieutenant scowled. "And doubly annoying that he had a medkit on him."

In response to the rare display of anger from the other woman, Julianna said, "Don't worry. Jared will pay. Grentham will pay. If the dwarves choose not to play along by hiring Worldspan, well, they'll pay, too."

Grentham pushed open the door to Jared's hospital room, satisfied with the attentiveness of the duo on guard outside it. His partner was sitting up in bed, flicking through television channels and looking bored. Grentham said, "Man, this is the life. Hang around, watch TV, get waited on hand and foot."

Jared snorted. "Want to trade? I'm down."

He shook his head. "No thanks. I dislike doctors and hate hospitals." He moved closer and lowered his voice. "Smith is dead."

A wide smile spread across his partner's face. "Really?"

"I wanted to tell you in person. He took a long drop with a sudden stop."

"Nice. And his partner?"

Grentham shrugged. "Had to divide and conquer. We'll deal with her later. Are you ready to get out of this place yet?"

Jared sighed and dropped the remote on his blanket-covered legs. "Doctors say a few more days before they can move me safely. Some of the stitching they do inside is delicate."

"They're lying. Just want you to pay extra to stay longer."

A laugh escaped his partner. "Could be, but I think I'll believe them on this, what with all that time spent in medical school."

Grentham's expression turned serious, and he gripped the rail on the edge of the hospital bed. "I don't think you're safe here."

Jared nodded. "I get it. You kicked the hornets' nest, and they'll be buzzing. I don't want to die because we decide to relocate me too soon, either."

"The doctors aren't thinking about portals. We could transfer you safely."

The other man shook his head. "Too much on the unknown side of the equation. Plus, the AI medical kit was single-use. I'm without a backup plan until I can get another, and that's going to take some serious effort. Let's play the odds and trust the docs, at least until it's vital that we don't."

Grentham scowled. *I don't have to like it, but it's his call.* "A second guard in here, then." It was a statement, not a question.

His partner acquiesced. "Sure. I can deal with that. As long as everyone understands I'm in control of the TV remote."

Grentham managed a laugh and reached into the backpack he'd brought along. He withdrew a small canister and handed it over. "Take a look at this in your spare time. It's an anti-magic emitter Smith tried against me. Worked really well, actually, but fortunately not for long. If it had lasted another thirty seconds or so, he would've been the one visiting you instead of me."

Jared turned it over in his hands, examining the outer casing. "I guess I can free up a little time from my sitcom-watching schedule. Thanks."

"Might be handy when we take on Worldspan again."

Jared's head snapped up. "You don't think that's over?"

Grentham scratched at his beard. "I can't imagine a future where our business with them is over. Even if it is on their end, it's not on mine. That wench needs to go down."

Jared chuckled. "What is it with you and her?"

"What was it with you and Smith?" Grentham shook his head. "I don't know, man. She infuriates me. And to have her thinking she's won? Hell no."

"Better make sure you prepare your travel plans in advance of that adventure."

He patted his partner on the shoulder. "They've been ready for weeks. I wonder if Reno could use a new security company. What do you think?"

Jared nodded. "Yeah. I'm coming around to the idea of putting Magic City in the rearview. Wouldn't you miss being part of the Council, a community leader, and all that?"

Grentham rolled his eyes. "Those people suck, especially since Elnyier's in charge. No, I think the next phase of my existence should be devoted to the pursuit of wealth and comfort. Wine, women, song, the whole nine yards."

Jared leaned back, his hands continuing to explore the canister. "Now that sounds like a plan, partner."

CHAPTER TEN

Ruby ducked under the swipe of the sword that sought her head. She whipped her blade around, tip pointed to the ground, to deflect the one aimed at her ankles. She knew better than to leap over it and give her opponent the opportunity to slam into her while her balance was compromised. Her foot lashed out in a kick, but the other woman danced nimbly back, twirling both blades in a flourish before stepping into a fighting stance.

Keshalla remarked, "Speed's not bad, but against two swords, a single blade is going to put you on the defensive most of the time."

Ruby scowled, but her teacher had spent the last twenty minutes demonstrating the truth of her words. Ruby tried again to send lightning through the sword at her mentor, but it fizzled out somewhere along the path. She growled in frustration and attacked, but Keshalla blocked her swing and circled her blade to redirect it, opening up Ruby's ribs for a stab.

Ruby intercepted it with a force-covered hand, earning

a dark look from her mentor. "Yeah, yeah, I need a real blocking option. I know. I'll ask Shentia for the dagger back or get a different one."

Keshalla attacked, and in between strikes, observed, "You might be better off with something like a sai, able to trap weapons rather than only stopping them. That would nullify part of your opponent's advantage in the two-swords-to-one scenario."

Ruby tried to send magic down the blade again and failed again. She sensed the beings within trying to speak to her and fell easily into the mental space she used to commune with them. Her design was present today, comfortable chairs set on a finely woven rug in the middle of an expansive grassland.

She retained a sense of her body's actions as it continued the battle against Keshalla, but time passed very differently in this place, allowing her ample opportunity for discussion. Shalia and Tyrsh were seated already, and Ruby claimed her chair facing them. She complained, "I can't seem to get it to work."

The female inhabitant of her sword, who today wore a bright blue gown that covered her from neck to ankles, replied, "Yet your ability to contact us has improved, as has your body's capacity to fight while you're here."

Tyrsh, dressed in tunic and trousers of a silvery gray, nodded agreement. "Things progress."

Ruby didn't miss that the pair had collectively chosen clothing in her house colors, a move that touched her more than she would have expected. The pleasant emotion lasted all of a heartbeat before a sardonic voice drawled, "You might be one of the dense ones."

She sighed and turned toward the sound. The Atlantean, as if he desired to be as different from the other two as possible, wore only a pair of bright scarlet shorts. His body was perfect, of course, since they all controlled how they looked in the shared space. Dark skin and muscles complemented the thick braids that fell past his shoulders. She said, "Come again?"

He laughed. "No, I'm not insulting your intelligence, although there's doubtless room to do so. What I mean is your mental shields are so resistant to opening that you can't achieve the proper connection with the sword unless you've submerged in it. So, like, you're dense."

Ruby turned to the sword's inhabitants, both of whom were nodding. "That makes sense to you?"

Shalia shrugged. "It's as good an explanation as any. We don't know why the skill eludes you. Given that we didn't believe it possible, we are far from expert."

With a sigh of annoyance at having to ask the artifact for anything, she said, "What's the solution?"

His confident grin begged for her to punch him. "The easiest one would be to always fight with your consciousness inside the sword. That will provide the connection you need and also make the twins over there *really* happy."

The sentient inhabitants of her sword vibrated with anger at the mockery the Atlantean sent their way. Ruby shook her head. "No. I have to keep my focus outside the sword. I'm not usually alone, and even when I am, I need to be more aware of what's going on around me than I can be from in here."

Tyrsh offered, "Shalia is correct. You are getting better at existing in both places simultaneously."

Ruby replied, "Even so."

The Atlantean said, "Then, blood."

She closed her eyes and shook her head in exasperation. "You're screwing with me now, right?"

He chuckled. "It would be *so* easy to do so, given your lack of knowledge. But no, I'm not. Power needs a channel through which to flow. You want to connect your sword to your power. Your touch isn't enough, which suggests a deeper connection of some kind is necessary."

"That involves blood; how?"

"Simple. Have a small pin put on your sword hilt, only large enough to pierce the skin. That will create a path the power can flow along. That could well be sufficient to allow you to cast through it."

She frowned. It made sense, although advice from the unwanted passenger lodged in her arm was inherently suspect. "And if it doesn't?"

He shrugged. "Cut off your hand and replace it with the sword?"

She growled, "If this doesn't work, I'm going to burn you in a fire."

His laughter *also* begged to be punched. "Do as you will. I always seem to survive and find a new host."

"Were you this annoying to the others?"

He countered, "They were far more intelligent. They chose a full partnership with me."

Ruby waved. "Begone." The Atlantean vanished, his laugh trailing behind him like the Cheshire cat's smile. She asked Tyrsh and Shalia, "Does what he says makes sense?"

The other woman replied, "It seems viable. Certainly, as

long as you can make the addition easily, without damaging the sword itself, it's worth a try."

Tyrsh added, "There's some risk to altering an artifact weapon. You'll need an expert. Perhaps consider finding a sharp edge to cut yourself on. Or maybe use the blade for that purpose. To test it, I mean."

Ruby nodded. "That's good advice. Thank you." She sent her consciousness spiraling back out of the safe space, and her teacher knocked the sword from her grip with a hard rap that sent pain vibrating through her fingers. "Ow. Unfair."

Keshalla laughed. "You weren't fully here. What's on your mind?"

She reached out with her force magic and pulled the fallen weapon back to her hand. "I was chatting with the sword and the artifact." She waggled her left arm to indicate the octopus tattoo and the magical item that lay underneath it. "About how to cast magic through the sword."

"Did you come up with something?"

She explained the plan the Atlantean had suggested. Keshalla frowned. "It certainly seems logical, but it's true that altering an artifact weapon is not a decision to be made lightly."

"Do you know someone who could do it?"

"Maybe."

Ruby nodded. "Well, I guess we should test it." Before she could think about it further, she transferred the sword to her left hand and nicked a finger on her right with the tip of the blade. She held it there and called for magic. Lightning wreathed the sword instantly, then sizzled out to slam into the shield her mentor had raised to defend herself. Ruby grinned. "Well, would you look at that?"

Keshalla shook her head. "You're incapable of taking anything slowly and carefully, aren't you?"

"Yep. Learned that from you."

The other woman sighed. "How can *you* be the leader of the Mist Elves?"

She laughed. "I'm just that amazing. Now, talk to me about people who might be able to customize this weapon. Then let's practice some more. This is fun."

CHAPTER ELEVEN

After dinner at her parents' house the next day, Ruby and the rest of her family moved into the study to discuss the impending event. Dralen said, "This isn't coming a moment too soon. People at Spirits have been tense since the moment she took over."

Her father nodded. "All the casino owners are feeling the pressure, and the tension is trickling down to the staff. Well, according to those who will talk to me, anyway. Rosalind is solidly in Elnyier's camp, so we aren't speaking at the moment."

Ruby sighed. "Guess we shouldn't have rescued her, then. Did you tell Elnyier what was coming?"

He shook his head. "No, but just about every member of the Council has a fatal case of loose lips, plus there aren't many reasons to call a special meeting. Hopefully, she won't find out enough in advance to stop tonight's vote."

Sinnia remarked, "It's not only Elnyier that's upsetting the other owners, though, is it?"

Rayar shook his head and picked up the tumbler of

whiskey from where it sat on the end table beside his wingback leather chair. "No, the damned Drow who's marauding in the streets has everyone tense as well."

Ruby asked, "Why?"

Her mother laughed. "Something you'll discover as you get older is that change becomes harder and harder to accept. As does unpredictability. That guy and his gang are chaos in a bottle."

Her father added, "One that gets uncapped entirely too often."

Morrigan stared at her, and Ruby could imagine the comments she'd like to make about the Hat being uncapped. She scowled, and her sister turned away to keep her grin from getting bigger. Ruby said, "So, they're reacting by worrying?"

Rayar replied, "Lots of worrying, yes. Some discussion of handing over operations to younger family members and getting some distance from the business. It's as if there's a sudden affliction of feeling old, or maybe inadequate to the moment."

Dralen added, "Plus, several used Aces for their security and have now had to hire Worldspan instead, based on the goings-on."

Her mother shook her head. "Foolish on both their parts, but Worldspan seems to have come out on top."

Ruby said, "I feel like there's more to that story, although I can't imagine what it is." *Other than the widow Sloane, if Grentham is right. I have no reason to think he isn't.*

Rayar shrugged. "Ultimately, it doesn't affect our family directly, except by adding pressure to the mix and forcing some personnel changes. Anyway, hopefully after tonight, things will be better."

Morrigan asked, "You have the votes?"

He sighed. "I believe I do, but I can't be sure. Those who weren't already behind Elnyier should be willing to vote against her. For Challen, I think it's because he doesn't like how she handled replacing Maldren. For Grentham, it's probably personal. Most things are with him. I should have the edge I need."

Ruby replied, "Once you're leader of the Council, what then?"

He laughed. "Why, expand our borders, take over anyone who tries to resist, and rule the world, of course."

They all joined in the mirth. Sinnia smiled at her husband and said, "Now there's the man I married."

Ruby shook her head. She hoped for the best but couldn't escape the thought that Elnyier was entirely smart enough to have seen this coming.

Most of the Council had assembled, or perhaps it was fairer to say that most of the surviving members of the original Council had gathered. Replacements for those who had fallen weren't yet named. Each group doing its version of the political infighting the Council was engaged in was the likeliest reason why. Ruby suspected that Elnyier had fanned those flames and blocked those who had chosen. Regardless, as soon as Grentham and Challen arrived to join Rayar, Elnyier, and Rosalind, they'd have a quorum, and the meeting would be able to begin.

The dwarf came through the door as if her thought had summoned him, looking surly. He glanced around the table, and his frown deepened. "Where's Challen? We need to get this show on the road. I have things to do."

Elnyier, clad all in black and sitting primly in her chair, offered him a thin smile and a venomous tone. "So sorry that Council business has interfered with your agenda, Grentham."

He laughed as he sat. "Removing the mask, huh? Probably about time since you weren't fooling anyone, anyway."

Rosalind countered, "You're one to talk. How long have you been bragging to us about the stability of your security company? Doesn't look too stable right now." *Okay, she's definitely on Elnyier's side. Ingrate.*

Grentham's face went flat. "You can knock us down, but have no fear. When we stand back up, we'll be ready to fight."

Elnyier made a point of looking down at her watch, then returned her gaze to the group. "I'm afraid we don't have a quorum. The loss of our comrades means everyone but one remaining would have to attend, and as you can see, neither Maldren nor Challen has arrived. Unfortunate."

Ruby was so occupied with the gnome's absence that she'd not taken notice of the fact that Maldren was also missing. *I didn't even think of him as part of the council. Too used to remembering him in charge, I guess. I'm sure Dad was counting on him.*

Rayar said, "I believe our rules give them some latitude. Ten minutes, isn't it?"

Elnyier gave her head a slight shake. "For special meetings like this one, actually, that rule doesn't apply. But, by all means, let us wait." Her confidence told Ruby that the result was preordained.

The next double handful of minutes passed excruciatingly slowly, the Council members glaring at each other in silence and Ruby doing her best not to fidget where she stood behind her father's chair. When the designated interval had come and gone, Elnyier shrugged. "We are adjourned. See you at the next regularly scheduled meeting. I'm sorry that my acquiescence to Rayar's request has wasted your time." She rose and exited in the room in a swirl of black skirts.

Ruby exploded the moment they were through the front door of their house, where no one could see or overhear them. "That woman is such an evil wench."

Her father nodded. "She really is. I thought we'd seen the worst of her, but the attitude she had on display tonight shows she's done pretending to be part of us. What's more concerning is that Maldren and Challen weren't there. I didn't speak to the healer, but I had every expectation that he would be present. Counted on it, in fact. To my knowledge, he's never missed a meeting."

He headed into the study, and Ruby followed him. "Maldren, on the other hand, I was positive would attend. I talked to him earlier today, and the plans were solid. Thought maybe him exercising his right to join the Council and vote would be something she wouldn't expect." He shook his head as he filled two glasses with a short drink of whiskey. "I fear one or both of them has met with misfortune."

She nodded. "I feel the same way. I'll grab Idryll and check on Challen. You do the same with Maldren. Take Morrigan with you. She can run information wherever it needs to go. Idryll can do the same for me."

Her father nodded as he set the untasted glasses on the table. "Be careful. There's no telling what she's up to."

Ruby turned and headed for the stairs. She called back over her shoulder, "I think we're safe in the kemana. She'd be foolish to try something here."

Her father's response reached her ears at the landing. "Only if you assume she's playing by anything like the same rules we are."

Ruby strode toward the door and opened it. "Come on, cat. We need to visit the doctor." She summoned a portal that would let her out on the street outside the healer's house. It was a destination she knew well.

Idryll stepped up beside her and asked, "Are you hurt?"

Ruby shook her head. "No. But if someone's messed with Challen, that someone is going to be hurt. Big time."

She extended her hand and used force magic to summon her sheathed sword into it, then strode through with Idryll close on her heels.

CHAPTER TWELVE

Ruby froze with her hand an inch away from the front door of Challen's small home and office. She listened attentively, seeking whatever had tweaked her instincts. Nothing was apparent, so she tried carefully inspecting the door. That, too, resulted in nothing.

She put her hand on the hilt of her artifact sword and whispered, "I could use any help you can give me." She made a careful effort to open her senses to the magic around her fully.

Normally, she maintained powerful barriers. It was an automatic habit Keshalla had instilled in her from the first day of their training. Without walls in place, a fight could be over before it began if an enemy was strong enough to roll her mind. She sensed wrongness on the entire door. "That's weird," she muttered.

Idryll asked, "What?"

Ruby shook her head slowly. "I honestly can't say. Only that something's strange about the door, and it feels like danger."

The shapeshifter replied, "The house has a chimney. Assuming there's no fire going, I could get in that way."

Her frown grew. "No, I want you near me." She considered her options and wished the small explosive devices weren't back in the bunker. Even though it would only take a couple of minutes to retrieve them, she was unwilling to invest the time. Her senses were screaming that something was wrong, and if Challen was hurt inside, she needed to get to him. "To hell with it. Come with me."

She retreated around the corner of the nearby house, where she wouldn't be in any potential trap's line of fire. Then she reached out with all her magical strength, grabbed the door with her force magic, and yanked. On the third pull, it came free, discharging a fireball into the street.

The moment the arcane flames had dissipated, Ruby ran in with her sword drawn, its sheath left behind on the ground to free up her other hand for magic. Challen's main room was the same as always, doubling as both living space and reception area for his healing business. She peered into the medical office first, fearing what might await her inside, but found nothing. Idryll said softly, "That door, to the left."

Ruby turned to her. Idryll's nostrils had flared, and her face held a sheen of sadness. *Dammit, Challen, please only be injured.* She opened the door and found the gnome lying peacefully in bed, his skin ashen and his body unmoving.

She extended her senses again, seeking traces of magic, but found none. An amateur examination came up with nothing useful. No wounds or other obvious causes of his passing were visible. *I'm not the right person for this job.* "Idryll, go get Shentia and bring her here, please."

It didn't take long for the Drow shopkeeper to arrive. She shook her head at the sight of the gnome. "This is unfortunate. I liked him very much."

Ruby nodded. "I did too. So I need to find out how he died. Normally, I'd ask the healer, but," she gestured helplessly at the body on the bed.

Shentia moved to examine it. "So, you figured a Drow would know about death?"

"No. I just don't have anyone else to trust outside my family."

The other woman looked over her shoulder at Ruby for a moment, then nodded. She turned back to her work, bending over to peer closely at him, then said, "Look here." Ruby stepped forward and examined the spot the Drow indicated. A small puncture wound was present on the side of his neck.

Anger swirled inside her. "Poison?"

Shentia straightened with a slight groan. "Almost certainly. I'm sorry to say, based on the way the skin around the injection responded and the black gums, it's likely a Drow poison."

Ruby gripped her sword harder until her fingers hurt, helping her to focus past her rage. "So Elnyier did this?"

"Not necessarily. The concoction's components are available everywhere, and the formula is probably somewhere on the Internet by now, given how much our people have integrated with humans."

"Still, it does seem quite the coincidence."

The other woman nodded. "It does. Moreover, if it was

Elnyier, she wanted you to know it. Or," she corrected herself, "wanted whoever found the body or was in charge of the investigation to know it."

Ruby said, "Thank you, Shentia. I have to talk to my father. Can you take care of this? I know it's a big ask."

The shopkeeper nodded. "As you said, trustworthy individuals are in short supply at the moment. I will see that our friend gets properly taken care of."

She portaled back to the house and hurried down the stairs to her father's study. He was pacing the room, with a visibly shaken Maldren sitting in one of the leather chairs. His guest spoke in a voice that trembled with something like fear, or rage, or a combination of the two.

"Elnyier made me stay away. She sent a lackey to me earlier, a Drow I don't know, and he showed me pictures of documents that could destroy my family. I have no idea where she got them. I can't even be sure they're real, but they looked it."

He drank from the glass in his hand before he resumed speaking. "It's something that started in my father's time. Apparently, he stole from someone he shouldn't have. It's not impossible. He was a bit of a rogue back then.

"The documents indicate that theft has continued, not a huge amount, but enough that we'd look guilty. You know what that would do to our standing with the rest of the casino owners." He shook his head. "When I find out whoever is inside my company making this happen, death will be too good for them."

Ruby exchanged glances with her father. She'd never seen him as ferociously angry as he appeared at that moment. Still, even at his most outraged, what he felt couldn't hold a candle to the molten lava that filled her stomach. She turned and headed for her sister's room, needing to take action before she exploded.

Fifteen minutes later, Ruby, Morrigan, and Idryll were in the bunker with Demetrius on comms. She pulled out her equipment belt and started refilling the materials she'd expended. Idryll and Morrigan busied themselves with their preparations.

Ruby said, "Something is going on with the Drow, and not only the Hat. Elnyier, too. Something big enough that it was worth killing Challen over." She paused to leash her anger yet again and forced the next words out through gritted teeth. "We need to find out what it is."

Morrigan replied, "How?" Her voice held no hint of amusement. It was as dark as Ruby had ever heard her sister sound, including when she talked about her kidnapping.

"We're going into Darkest Night."

Idryll asked, "Again, how?"

Ruby scowled at the grenade that wasn't fitting into its slot properly. *Come on, damn it, work with me.* "The hard way. We'll get in from the roof and go down in disguise or under an illusion or both. It's not subtle, and we'll need to be sure we have exit routes ready at all times. We don't have time to infiltrate quietly."

She'd expected her sister to argue, to try to be the voice of caution. Instead, Morrigan simply asked, "When?"

"As soon as we're sure Elnyier's not there. I want the

opportunity to see what secrets it holds without dealing with her, too. She's smart, and we're better off splitting up these challenges. D, do what you need to do. Hack reservation lists, get drones up, whatever. Find us a window."

He responded, "On it."

Ruby instructed the others, "Bring everything you need and pack extras, too. We have to assume every Drow we see is working against us in that place."

Morrigan replied, "Got it." Her voice softened a touch. "Are you okay?"

She shook her head. "No. I'm really not. And I won't be until we finish with this. So get cracking."

CHAPTER THIRTEEN

Ruby, Morrigan, and Idryll crouched on the rooftop of the casino nearest Darkest Night. The Drow casino's hotel tower was on a level with them, and Demetrius' drones provided an image of their target from high enough above to avoid notice. *If they are spotted, well, other drones are around here all the time, so they won't necessarily be alarming.* She said, "I see two sentries making a circuit of the perimeter. Looks like they have headsets and microphones."

Demetrius confirmed, "That's what I've got, too. They're encrypted, but it doesn't look that complicated. I should be in shortly."

Ruby replied, "You'll be able to pretend to be them?"

"Child's play. As soon as I understand what their confirmation routine is like, we'll be good to go."

She nodded and squashed her desire to charge into action. "Waiting on your word." She pulled her drone from the compartment on the back of her belt, unfolded its fans, and set it on the rooftop. She tapped the button on the controller on her arm to launch the preflight diagnostic, and everything came up green, the same as when she'd checked it earlier at the bunker. "This can get close without being seen, and it carries a knockout gas capsule. That should take care of one."

Morrigan nodded. "I'll handle the other once we portal into the gap created by you taking out the first. Good plan."

Ruby asked, "D, any other security on the roof?"

"Cameras, heat sensors, the usual. If you wait until I'm all the way into their system, I'll be able to block any alerts. Otherwise, you'll need to deal with them."

Ruby replied, "We'll wait. We can't risk tipping people off that we're here. Too many of them and not enough of us. We'll have to be extra careful inside, and you'll need to have exit routes for us ready to go. We can't allow them to catch us because I can't afford for them to identify me. None of us can."

It was an eternal five minutes before Demetrius announced, "I'm into their comms and the casino's alarm systems. You're free to operate. The only way they'll be able to detect you is if they have someone human watching the feed." The cameras' fields of view appeared in her display as wide cones that moved slowly across the rooftop. Their pattern offered two points where they could act with minimal risk. *Not bad coverage, really.*

Morrigan said, "I've got the cameras, no worries."

Ruby replied, "You're that sure of your new trick, are you?"

"It's not a trick. It's complicated illusion magic, something you wouldn't understand. Yes, I'm entirely confident."

She muttered a response under her breath as she

piloted the drone across the space between the buildings. Her mask's left lens showed the view from the small camera mounted in its nose. The structures caused the air currents to move strangely between them, and the wind buffeted her tiny craft. She compensated, brought the drone into position, and triggered the payload.

The deployment function operated perfectly. The Drow sentry dropped, fortunately away from the edge rather than toward it. She had been ready to try to catch him magically, but it would've been a challenge. The backup plan had been for Morrigan to attempt to portal him in midair. Overall, it was best that they didn't have to use either option.

Her sister conveyed them to the other roof and launched an arrow in a short arc to take out the second sentry. Demetrius guided Ruby into the spot where he wanted his network enhancer placed, and she stuck its adhesive feet onto the side of a piece of HVAC machinery. Access to the roof was through a trapdoor and ladder, and she led the others down into a workspace filled with control apparatus and supplies for repairing the stuff on the roof. It was noisy enough to cover their sounds and lacked surveillance equipment, making it perfect for them. Morrigan asked, "Okay, where to?"

Ruby hadn't been sure exactly what she wanted to accomplish in the casino, only that she had to put a crimp in Elnyier's plans, whatever they were. Now she knew. *The best way to mess her up is to hit her where it hurts.* "Elnyier's office."

Idryll said, "Ah, that's why you had to be positive she wasn't here."

Sure, as far as you know. "I'm not always stupid, see?" They found a set of lockers with coveralls in them, and Morrigan and Ruby created perfect illusions of the clothes to cover their costumes. Ruby added one for Idryll and gave them each Drow features, while Morrigan did the same for her face. She asked, "You can still handle the cameras?"

Her sister replied, "As long as I know where they are."

Demetrius fed a schematic to their lenses with that information, as well as other useful tidbits like locked doors and what areas had extra surveillance on them. He warned, "Guard patrols are present on every floor. Their patterns seem random."

Ruby replied, "Remember, we belong here. We're simply three workers doing our thing if anyone notices us." She'd planned to move under a veil but abandoned that notion, deciding on the spot that their illusory costumes would be sufficient to handle any encounter. She grabbed a wheeled trashcan from a corner, then handed a vacuum to Idryll and a broom to Morrigan. "What's our best route?"

"Service elevator. I wouldn't get off on the executive floor. Go one above and work your way down. You'll want to do that carefully, though, because the security office is on that level."

As they walked along the hallway, Morrigan murmured, "Are you sure that's the best idea?"

Demetrius replied, "Yeah. They'll be more on guard against infiltration from below than above. Problems are more likely to come from that direction."

Idryll said, "We should create a distraction, maybe."

Ruby shook her head. "Nope, we're only normal

people." She nodded at another coverall-wearing worker who passed them in a hurry. "Looks like the workers here are tense. Probably the supervisors are tough on the brutal side. Elnyier's a wench, so those beneath her likely are too."

They made it to the fourth floor and passed the security office unchallenged, then followed Demetrius's directions to a break room. They used illusion to get back out without appearing to have done so and took the staircase down a level, the infomancer opening the electronic locks along their path.

A few minutes later, they were on the floor with the executive offices. They were appropriately dark, given that it was one in the morning. Elnyier's office didn't have a normal lock but featured a handprint instead. Ruby said, "D, little help."

He replied, "Can't do it remotely. You have to open it up and use the chip I gave you. It'll probably short out the panel."

"Can't be helped." He'd supplied a small data drive with lock picking software on it as a backup plan. The next-level backup option was a generic electronic lock pick that was part of her standard gear, but she doubted it would've worked on this panel. She pulled out the compact toolkit from her belt and selected the smallest levers, using them to separate the faceplate from the wall and get at the connections behind it.

The panel came apart with four screws, giving her access to the computer board inside it. Attaching the chip took a little improvisation and some of the wire she always carried, but a moment later, the door unlatched. She took the drive out and put the panel back so no one would notice the intrusion until someone tried to use it.

Idryll observed, "Now she'll know we were here. Weren't we trying to be secret?"

Ruby nodded. "Yeah, that was the original plan. But you know, she sent us a message with her choice of poison. Assuming that was her, which I do. Just sending her one back."

The office interior was no different from any other executive suite she'd been in, except that it was spotless. They split up to examine the place, but no papers were left out, no computer rested on the desk, and the only storage container in the room was a safe hidden inside a credenza.

Morrigan observed, "Well, that's annoying. How paranoid do you have to be to lock up your computer inside your locked office inside your locked casino?"

Ruby replied, "It's not a bad idea. Secure your laptops when not in use."

Her sister grudgingly admitted, "Yeah, you're right. I should probably suggest that."

Ruby nodded. "Agreed. That doesn't help us at the moment."

Idryll said, "I think I have something that will, though."

She turned and asked, "What?"

Her companion pointed at the floor. "A subtle wear pattern in the carpet, as though Elnyier took one path more often than she did others. There's a similar line between the door and the desk, but this leads straight to a wall."

They examined it, and Morrigan said, "Look around for a switch or something."

It took several minutes of searching before Idryll found it on the underside of the desk. When she pushed the button, a small panel released in the wall, barely high enough to walk through and so narrow that only one person could fit at a time, and only if they went through sideways. Ruby swung it open and peered inside. "It's a dark shaft going down. I think I see a light at the bottom."

Morrigan replied, "Like the one into the kemana? Think it goes there?"

She shook her head. "I really doubt it. She could portal there. This needs to be someplace she couldn't necessarily reach that way, or its presence and use don't make sense. I'll jump down and see what's going on."

Her sister said, "If she can't portal there, there may be anti-magic in use. You try it, and you could go splat."

Ruby sighed. "Yeah, you have a point. I'm sure I would've thought of that before I jumped." *Hopefully.* "Anyway, let's see what's up." She unpacked her drone again and flew it down, finding that the shaft did indeed end in a lighted space. She didn't take the drone to the floor, not wanting to reveal their presence.

While she'd been working, Morrigan had been unspooling the grapnel from her belt. She secured it to the handle on the safe, which wasn't about to budge, and gathered the line in her hand. "I'll go down, and you can follow. The cable can only support one of us at a time."

"Then I'll go first."

Morrigan countered, "It's my line."

"What are you, three? I'm the better fighter in close quarters, which is what's probably down there."

Her sister grumbled but handed over the cable. Ruby

said, "Okay, be ready to follow." She let herself down carefully, with the line wrapped around her back to manage the friction and speed of her descent. When she got above the lighted portion, she released the rope, falling the last eight feet and landing cleanly in a crouch.

Two Drow guards in front of her lurched into motion, and the sound of snapping bowstrings came from both sides. Ruby dove forward in a roll. "Outnumbered. Get the hell down here. Also, you were right about the anti-magic."

CHAPTER FOURTEEN

Ruby's sudden dive caused the bolts to miss, and by the time she returned to vertical, four knives in the hands of two Drow were coming in at her. "Probably poisoned blades," she muttered as she braced to take them on. All four guards were in light battle armor, and the pair nearest her held the daggers.

She had an instant to notice that the other duo was already reloading their pistol crossbows, then she was dodging and ducking as she drew her sword to engage the knife-wielders. Idryll plummeted into the room, hit the floor, rolled, and threw herself at one of the crossbow guards.

She had no idea how her companion had convinced Morrigan to let her go first, but her arrival was timely in more ways than one. The nearest guard shifted his attention away for a heartbeat at the tiger-woman's appearance, and Ruby shoved her sword above the armor plate guarding his thigh, stabbing deep into the muscle.

He grabbed the wound and fell with a cry, and she

aimed her backstroke at the other one's head. He dropped rather than trying to block it, and she snapped out a kick at him. He positioned his dagger quickly, and her booted foot came down on the point. It penetrated the leather sole and the flesh it contained. Ruby screamed as she pulled the leg back, unable to bear the thought of setting her foot down as agony washed through it.

Her foe grinned at his success for a moment, right up until the flying body Idryll had hurled across the room slammed into him and propelled him sideways into the wall with a loud *crunch*. Ruby hopped on one foot and yanked the dagger out of the other, then slapped the healing capsule on her shoulder harder than she needed to. The burning pain receded as the potion did its work.

In the meantime, Idryll had wrestled the pistol crossbow away from the last sentry, and Morrigan had arrived. It took only a few minutes more to knock out and bind the guards. Ruby tentatively lowered her foot to the floor. "I didn't hear them communicating with anyone, did you?"

Idryll shook her head. "They didn't say anything, only attacked. Must not have communications down here. Stand around and keep an eye on the elevator for eight hours until relieved, I guess. Boring."

Morrigan asked, "How's the foot?"

Ruby replied, "It's fine. Healing capsule. Either it wasn't a poisoned knife, or the potion took care of it." *I hope.* "Let's see what they were guarding." Another handprint panel showed in the wall between where the guards had stood, and she disabled it in short order. The door opened to reveal a large portal shimmering in midair, with a darkened cavern beyond it. "I'm not sure what I was expecting, but this definitely isn't it."

Morrigan said, "Yeah. Weird."

Idryll's voice was full of conviction. "We should *not* go through there. There's surely danger through there. *Dangerous* danger. You're aware of that, right?"

Ruby nodded. "Totally aware, but we're going to do it, anyway."

Her sister replied, "You go first. If I don't see you on the other side, I'll assume it sent you to the World In Between. I'll go home and tell our parents you said I could have your stuff."

She snarked, "Thanks for being such a team player, *Barb*." She sheathed her sword and rolled her neck, which gave a soft *crack* as it popped. "D, probably about to go out of contact. Try not to worry about us."

Morrigan replied, "He's part of the stuff I get to have if you die, so we're clear."

The joke didn't penetrate her focus as Ruby stepped through the portal. She didn't end up anywhere other than where the opening had appeared to lead, so the others followed her through a moment later.

Idryll frowned. "We're on Oriceran."

Morrigan asked, "Really?"

"Can't you feel it?"

Ruby replied, "No, but I believe you. Any idea where on Oriceran?"

The shapeshifter shook her head. "Nope. Certainly doesn't seem familiar to me. This stone looks nothing like the mountain, though."

Ruby squinted ahead, trying to make out more detail in

the dim illumination the lighting fixtures in the tunnel provided. "If we're stereotyping, it makes sense that we're underground. Drow eyes are pretty good in the dark, yeah?"

Idryll said, "As far as I know. Our lenses aren't working."

She'd noticed the same thing. "Technology is probably suspect here unless it has some sort of magical component to it. Don't depend on it."

"Claws are always the best option."

Ignoring her companion, Ruby led the way along the corridor. Now that they had access to magic again, casting appropriate veils to hide them from view, quiet the sounds they made, and conceal their heat signatures was easy. The tunnel led to a staircase with another pair of guards standing at the bottom. They passed between them in single file, leaving the sentries unaware they'd failed their primary task.

The stairs led to a door, and after listening carefully to detect what might be beyond it, Ruby cracked it. Morrigan used her camera trick to hide their movement from anyone on either side of the doorway. The place immediately felt familiar to Ruby. "This is a lot like the castle in the middle of the kemana. The blocks seem to be the same size, although a different material and the hallways feel identical."

Idryll looked around speculatively. "Probably a standard template for them all. Why redo work if you don't have to?"

Morrigan whispered, "Or work at all, right? Spoken like a cat."

"Shut it."

Ruby hissed, "Both of you shut it. Focus." Even though their voices wouldn't carry, thanks to the veil, she found it difficult to maintain her calm with their antics. The anger she felt over Challen's death hadn't abated a bit. Instead, it grew with each passing hour. They penetrated farther into the castle, evading guard patrols and peering into the chambers they passed. Her frustration increased with each step as they found nothing out of the ordinary. The place was a base of some kind filled with Drow.

Morrigan asked, "Do you think this is where Elnyier lives? Is this her family?"

Ruby replied, "Might be. No real way to tell. Could be one family, could be many. Could be a clan, could be a gang, hell, could be an employment center for gigs on Earth, for all we know."

They came upon a large room that held an oversized door guarded by two sentries. Several more armored Drow were present in the chamber, standing along the walls, looking bored. The trio huddled in a vacant corner, and Ruby whispered, "Any ideas?" The others had none, and she didn't either. "Dammit. It sucks to come this far and not find anything definitive."

She shook her head and sighed. "Well, I guess we learned a lot of Drow are down here, and presumably they're loyal to Elnyier. That's more than we knew earlier, but it's certainly not all that useful." She pulled a locator out of her belt pouch and stuck it on the wall. "I don't know if these will work, but no harm in dropping a few in inconspicuous spots on our way. Let's get out of here."

They retraced their steps, but as they descended the

staircase back into the cavern, an unexpected sight greeted them: the Hat, with a pair of Drow behind him. The shock of seeing him caused Ruby to stumble, and her veil couldn't conceal the extra noise. An instant later, their magical concealment had been dispelled, and they were face-to-face with their foe. He backpedaled quickly and shouted, "Sound the alarm. Intruders. Kill them."

Morrigan was already drawing an arrow from her quiver as their illusory invisibility fell. She released it, and it sped forward at the guard on the right-hand side that had accompanied the Hat. It struck, and the force burst detonated from it, sending him flying to scrape against the wall and land in a sprawl.

Their target, since clearly if the Hat was here, they needed to capture him, danced adroitly over his fallen escort. She drew another force arrow and aimed it at the ceiling above him, hoping it would blast away his retreat. As it left the bowstring, she realized how stupid that was for a variety of reasons. Fortunately, it failed to collapse the tunnel on their heads or separate them from the way back to Earth.

She imagined she could portal home without a problem under normal circumstances, but there was no telling what sort of counterspells the Drow might have guarding their sanctuary. Finding herself in the World In Between because she'd been stupid and cut off their primary escape route would be a decidedly bad end. *Ruby would never let me forget that one for as long as we lived. Which, there, probably wouldn't be very long.*

She collapsed the bow and shoved it back into its holster, stepping forward to engage the Drow that had been guarding the stairs on her side. Her right fist lashed out, headed for his jaw, but he brought his dagger up and blocked the punch with the crosspiece. Her metal knuckles meeting his metal weapon sent pain through her wrist.

The other nearby guard stabbed a blade at her, and she covered her hand with force and slapped it down. The knife scraped along her protective barrier when he turned it in response to her move. She spun as if she would deliver a roundhouse kick but rammed her knee into him instead. He twisted enough to take the blow on muscle rather than on his ribs. *Damn, he's good.* She blocked another stab from the same weapon and jerked her hand back as the one he'd used to block with scraped along her arm.

Her armor held. However, his dagger was sharper than usual because its touch left a huge gouge behind. Morrigan decided to abandon finesse and blasted him with a burst of force, knocking him back a few steps. He must've called upon his magic to blunt the impact, though, since he didn't go as far as she'd hoped. On the positive side, one of his daggers fell to the ground.

She drew her left knife and attacked, but he used her tactic against her, calling up a force shield to intercept it. She gritted her teeth and pushed in at him, knowing she'd take some damage in exchange for what she had planned.

Sure enough, his knee rammed up into her ribs as she closed, but she was ready for it and continued, smashing into him and bringing her right hand down at his temple.

Her stun knuckles failed to snap, but the impact still dazed him. She slammed his head back against the wall, and he slumped to the ground. Panting, she checked around for danger, then sheathed her blade and grabbed her bow.

Idryll had responded to the sight of the Hat with a happy shout and launched herself at him. One of his guards interposed himself. She shifted form in mid-leap, landing on him as a tiger rather than a humanoid. Her weight was enough to drive him back and to the ground, and he frantically tried to stab her sides.

She transformed back, and his blows scraped her ineffectively, having aimed at a different spot. She snapped her forehead into his, but it failed to knock him out as she'd hoped. Instead, he smashed a knee up into her side and flipped her off him. She twisted and rolled, then banged into the far wall of the corridor as she rose to her feet.

He threw a knife at her, and she batted it aside contemptuously. His free hand didn't cast the spell she'd expected was coming and instead dipped to his belt. She was already spinning away as the darts flew, two of which embedded themselves in the wall beside her. The third scraped across her skin but didn't penetrate. She immediately felt the burn of poison, but it was a dull thing. *Probably wasn't deep enough to get it in there. Let's hope, anyway.*

She wouldn't change form again for fear that if poison was present, she'd draw it in further as part of the shift. Instead, she slashed out with her claws, only to be intercepted by the edge of his blade. He'd produced yet another knife from somewhere and stabbed at her, but she blocked down with her other hand and twisted, scraping her claws along his forearm. His armor held, mostly, although he did make a noise as if she'd at least caused him some pain.

In her peripheral vision, their target was turning to run down the corridor, and she spotted more people inbound from that direction. Her keen hearing picked up more coming from the other side as well. *Can't be delicate, too dangerous. Besides, we're not on Earth, so Alejo's rules don't apply.*

She stabbed both sets of claws into her foe's chest, and while he managed to get his arms in the way momentarily, she leapt into the air and kicked her feet backward to push herself off the wall. Her claws sank through his arms and into his torso, and his daggers dropped from nerveless fingers.

Idryll landed and ripped her claws out with a twist, ensuring he would bleed to death before any could help him. She called, "Incoming from both sides. We need to get out of here."

When Ruby didn't reply, she snapped her head around to see what had become of her partner. The look of fury that twisted Ruby's face was something she'd never seen her wear before, and if she weren't an ally, it would have scared the hell out of her.

CHAPTER FIFTEEN

Ruby's head snapped around to look first toward Idryll, then back the way they'd come. The guard she'd fought was down at her feet, but more were boiling in from all directions. Their quarry was precariously close to escaping her again. She willed her magic to keep him from getting away, and a reddish-purple haze exploded across her vision and crashed through her brain.

She fell to her knees as the artifact in her arm burned in a triumphant agony as it took advantage of her moment of weakness. Tentacles boiled out of it, shadow made solid, wrapping around the necks of the nearest Drow and squeezing or slamming them into the walls. One snagged the Hat's feet and yanked them out from underneath him.

Sounds became strangely muffled, and the space surrounding her was still and pure as if diamond encased her, and no one could penetrate it to hurt her. She couldn't reach for her sword because her free hand maintained the protective defense around her. Attacks slammed against it from all directions as the Dark Elves sought to stop the tentacles that threatened them at the source.

No matter how many enemies she removed from the fight, more appeared to replace them. Blades hammered on her shield, but none got through. She whispered the command word for her pendant, and another layer of safety wrapped around her, the shadow barrier somehow finding an affinity with the tentacles coming out of her arm, the two vibrating in harmony.

Inside her mind, the experience was almost like watching a movie. Her will had called forth the magic and imbued it with the mission of defeating the Drow and preventing their quarry from escaping. Now, it functioned more or less on its own while she watched the horror film unspool before her.

The tentacles grew sharp edges, and blood flowed. Enemies shouted and pointed, but none of their attacks could reach her. Idly, she wondered if the artifact was trying to get her killed so it could move on to another being. However, in that place and time, the concern that should've accompanied the idea failed to materialize.

Her magic protected her from blades and spells, and it was doubtful any of the Drow would be carrying anti-magic bullets. The idea of a Dark Elf with a pistol made her laugh. That did raise a slight worry in her mind since she'd encountered that situation before. *Am I going crazy? Is this what insanity feels like?*

Through the tumult, she sensed Idryll's touch on her shields. The tentacles didn't redirect to attack her companion, but neither did her protections allow the shapeshifter in. She mumbled, "Protect Mo," but didn't know if she'd done it for real or only imagined saying it.

Her eyes focused on the Hat, who was being dragged inexorably toward her. He'd devoted his efforts to protecting himself from the booted feet of combatants as he moved unwillingly through their battles.

Several Drow had engaged the tentacles rather than getting trapped by them. Each one they hacked into pieces sent pain shooting through her body, violent enough to make her gasp with each chop. New ones emerged instantly as the artifact drew on her resources to create them.

She imagined that her veins and arteries had become shadow conduits, that the Atlantean magic was pulling the very life out of her to fuel its vicious attack. It seemed like she should care about that, but it felt very far away.

A *creak* from above caught her attention, and she looked up to see the ceiling buckling over her head. Her sister entered her view, using her magic to redirect the stones away from Ruby. She shook her head. "Save yourselves. I've got this." When the stone stopped falling, her sister took up a position off to her right, daggers whirling to keep the Drow away from her kneeling form.

She presumed Idryll was behind her, guarding against the attacks from that direction. Concern for her companion, that she was out of sight and Ruby didn't know if she was okay, broke through the haze in her brain. She turned her head from side to side but couldn't see the shapeshifter.

The tendrils drew back a little, their complete aggression transforming into a mix of attack and defense. The

Hat remained bound, and by the shouts of pain that came from him, the tentacles around his feet had grown barbs as well. *Good. Serves you right, bastard.*

Anger warred with concern as she forced herself to rise. With her balance slightly compromised, the continuing attacks from the Drow all around buffeted her. She growled in annoyance.

She imagined a movie scene where someone spun in a circle and decapitated all the surrounding opponents in one strike. Suddenly the ends of the tendrils whirled like tiny saws, the sharpened barbs chopping into flesh and through bone wherever they encountered an enemy.

Ruby turned and found that Idryll was holding her own, but the reinforcements continued to flow. She sucked in a breath, and all the tentacles withdrew into her arm. Then she thrust the limb forward, and they erupted out of it together, spiraling around one another to form a huge, solid cone. It slammed into the roof above the door, and that part of the cavern caved in from the impact, dropping rocks onto the staircase and destroying it, then filling the opening with stone.

She turned and released the tendrils again, mowing through the remaining enemies on the other side. When the suffocating rage faded and she started to feel again, it was only her, Idryll, Morrigan, and the Hat still functional. Dozens of bodies littered the floor, injured, dead, dying. She didn't know which, and the purplish-red haze in her brain wouldn't let her care. The tentacles reached out and yanked the Drow leader to his feet, and she strode forward and punched him in the face. She expected pleasure but got nothing.

Morrigan shouted, and her voice managed to penetrate the buzzing in Ruby's ears. "Energy potion."

Ruby nodded, thinking that a boost would be good right about then. She slapped the capsule on her shoulder and ice flowed through her. The surge cleared her thoughts for only an instant, but she used it to grab her sword and pull the blade free. Tyrsh and Shalia entered her mind and assisted her in pushing back the artifact's influence. The tendrils receded, the Hat fell to the floor, dazed, and Ruby dropped to her knees again.

Idryll's arms were immediately around her, drawing her back to her feet. The shapeshifter said, "We have to get out of here, and we have to do it now.

Ruby muttered, "Don't portal from here. Dangerous." Her limbs felt like lead, and she could barely move them.

Morrigan replied, "I know. We've got you." Her sister yanked the Drow up again and wrapped a zip tie around his hands, binding them behind his back. They led the way, and Ruby followed blindly, guided by her companion. The battle continued in her brain, the artifact pushing against her sword's inhabitants, trying to reassert control. However, they'd reached a stalemate, and no more tentacles emerged from her arm.

They passed through the portal, back into the basement of Darkest Night. She had no idea how much time had gone by, but the guards were still as they'd left them, down and unconscious. Ruby slumped against the wall as Idryll joined her sister to locate the anti-magic emitters and dealt with them. Then Morrigan opened a portal to the receiving room at the bunker and pushed the Drow through it. When he appeared on the other side, the three of them followed. Ruby managed to mutter, "Give him to Andrews, anonymous," before she fell into darkness.

She awoke with a start, thrashing to guard against the horde of Drow surrounding her. Idryll's "Shh" arrived an instant before the shapeshifter's strong arms wrapped around her. Ruby calmed and realized she was in her bed at her parents' house. She said, "I don't suppose that was all a horrible nightmare."

Her companion's voice was soothing. "No. It was real. On the upside, you ended the threat against the humans in Magic City. That counts for a lot. That's not even the best thing."

Idryll's tone made it clear she wanted Ruby to ask, so she did. "What's the best thing?"

The tiger-woman pulled her over onto her back and knelt beside her. She now wore the hat she had coveted. Ruby broke into laughter, or tears, or both. Her voice caught as she said, "I killed all those people."

Idryll shook her head. "The artifact you never wanted in the first place got the best of you and used you to kill all those people. There's a difference there, and you need to remember it. You are not responsible. If anyone is, it's the Hat, and Elnyier, and bloody Rhazdon, way back when."

She heard the words, felt the truth in them, and accepted them. Something in her chest loosened. *Still going to have nightmares about that for a long time, though.* "Where is he?"

Idryll grinned. "The Hatless?" Ruby managed a laugh.

"We handed him over to Andrews like you said. Morrigan also told Alejo we did so. I imagine there was much rejoicing."

Ruby frowned. "You've been watching Monty Python?"

The other woman nodded. "One of the best things humans have ever created, in my opinion."

She sighed. "Okay, help me up. I need to talk to my father."

CHAPTER SIXTEEN

Ruby didn't get to talk to Rayar immediately. Her rest had taken her into the middle of the afternoon, and he was away at work. She had no desire to go to Spirits, felt that she'd be fine with spending a week or two in her bedroom relaxing. The artifact, or the battle, or *something*, had left her feeling hollow inside.

At some point, we have to see if those locators give us anything. But we don't have to do it right now. She had dinner in her room, rather than joining her parents, but found them in the study having a nightcap afterward. Her father said, "You look exhausted."

Ruby nodded. "I took one of Daphne's energy potions, then wound up missing out on sleep to work on some technomancy projects. That bill is pretty harsh when it comes due."

Her mother chuckled, seeming happy. "It's good that you're focusing on the important stuff, starting your business."

Rayar countered, "She has a business."

Ruby knew he meant at Spirits, but her mind instantly went to her role as defender of Magic City. *Yeah, I do, and I guess it's not going to get done if I hide here and rest.* She asked, "What's the news in town?"

Her father smacked his hands together. "The Drow that was leading the anti-human movement has been captured."

"Sheriff Alejo?"

He shook his head. "The Paranormal Defense Agency. I guess all their surveillance and whatnot finally proved useful."

Yeah, sure. When cows fly. "Did they find out why he was doing it?"

"Andrews reported to the Council that he was working on his own and simply wanted to rectify what he saw as an injustice in the city."

Ruby ground her teeth together. *The bastard didn't give up Elnyier. I guess I should've figured that would happen. Dammit.* "He had to have support. Any sign of who might have been helping him?"

Her father shook his head again. "No. But the fact that he was Drow has created problems for Elnyier on the Council. She's being blamed for not taking care of the situation herself, both by the people she leads and by the other Council members. I've pushed those whose leaders we lost to name a replacement quickly, and I think we'll be able to vote her out at the next regularly scheduled meeting."

Ruby felt a touch of relief, even though that wasn't nearly punishment enough for the other woman. "Excellent. I don't suppose that the Hat," she stumbled, then continued, "-wearing Drow confessed to being involved in Challen's death?"

Sinnia interrupted, "That is so sad. I really liked him."

"I did too."

Her father answered the original question, saying, "No, at least not that they've told us. I'm not sure they would share that regardless since a formal investigation still lies ahead. Normally the Council would oversee that, but obviously there's too much suspicion for that to happen right now. Eventually, we'll have to find someone who can look into it properly."

Ruby sighed. "I guess that will have to do. At least he's off the streets, right?" Her parents nodded, and Ruby headed back to her room. She flopped on the bed with a sigh when she got there. "The Hat didn't talk. Which means Elnyier gets to continue as she has been, although Dad says the Council will probably vote her out of leadership."

Idryll replied, "That's not cool. Maybe the PDA will do something about her?"

Ruby sighed. "The only ones who know he was connected to Elnyier, aside from being seen on a date or two, is us. If we admit we were there, we might get blamed for all the Drow that died." Her jaw locked up, and she worked it slowly, letting the stress dissipate. "That's certainly not something we want."

Idryll sat up and pulled her knees to her chest, wrapping her arms around them. "Do you think there's a danger of reprisal?"

Ruby sat up as well and turned to face her. "Against the persons unknown who invaded Darkest Night and the Drow caverns? Definitely, if they figure out who it is. I don't think there's any reason they will, though. We were careful. Still, extra vigilance for a while wouldn't be a bad idea."

Ruby twisted to lie back down, then caught sight of something across the room. She swung her legs out of bed instead and padded over to the wardrobe. On it was a ribbon similar to the one that Keshalla used to summon her to Oriceran, but with a wide gold band woven through it, setting off the blue and silver of her house colors. She asked, "Did you notice who left this here?"

Idryll replied, "No. I wasn't aware it was there. I might have been napping." She didn't sound in the least ashamed of that fact.

Ruby shook her head. "You're such a cat."

"You say that like it's a bad thing, rather than the pinnacle of existence, which is what it really is."

A real smile broke out on her face, and Ruby laughed in a mixture of pleasure and relief that she still could. "Well, we're being summoned to Oriceran. Time to get a move on."

She gathered her weapons, wondering why Keshalla had changed the ribbon but not particularly worried about it, and they stepped through to her house on the other planet. Her mentor was waiting in the living room and rose at their arrival. Ruby said, "Nice ribbon."

Keshalla smiled. "Your representative at the castle gave it to me. You're needed there in some official capacity."

She frowned. "They're using you as a messenger service?"

Her teacher laughed. "Don't sweat it. I volunteered. I'd rather have the number of people who know how to portal into your bedroom stay small."

Idryll replied, "That makes sense."

Ruby snorted. "Yeah, they might interrupt one of your endless naps."

Keshalla shook her head at them. "Portal, or walk?"

Ruby still had a core of unpleasant emotion writhing in the center of her stomach. Her feelings vacillated wildly from moment to moment, mirth to remorse, worry to confidence. "I think a walk would be best unless we're in a hurry."

"She didn't say, so I presume not."

"Yet you used the knot that said to get here quickly."

Keshalla chuckled. "Well, I'm not sure, am I? It seemed like the right choice."

As they walked through the mystics' village, it was strange to see so few of them about. Probably a fourth of their usual number still worked at maintaining their gardens, fixing up their buildings, and doing the normal daily tasks. The castle must've occupied far more of them than Ruby had expected for this many to be missing.

They entered her newest home and found the former messenger, now the castle's seneschal, waiting for them. She wore a formal dress that had an almost military styling to it, in the same blue, silver, and gold of the ribbon. Tirina nodded, deeply enough to be nearly a bow. "*Mirra*. It's good to see you again."

"And you, especially since you were ready to leave me for dead in the commune chamber." The other woman's eyes flicked to Keshalla, and Ruby said, "I trust her with everything. You can too."

Keshalla commented mildly, "So you abandoned my protégé to potential death?"

Tirina shrugged. "It worked out fine. Besides, I certainly wasn't going to get trapped in there with her."

Idryll laughed. "Good plan. Spend too much time around her, and you start to go a little crazy."

Ruby retorted, "And apparently become a somnambulist."

The shapeshifter frowned. "I'm going to look up the meaning of that word. If it means what I think it means, I get a training bout with you. Claws permitted."

Ruby chuckled. "Done." She turned to her seneschal. "So, why was I needed?"

"A petition has arrived. Two parties have a dispute they haven't been able to resolve by themselves. They've requested your assistance.

Ruby frowned. "It's a bad time. I'm not at my best."

The other woman shrugged. "It's a responsibility you swore to uphold. Bad day, good day, doesn't matter."

Ruby sighed. *There's no bend in you at all, is there, woman?* She straightened her shoulders and lifted her chin. "You're right. Where are they?"

Tirina smiled. "They will be here tomorrow, before midday."

She frowned suspiciously. "You did that on purpose. Made me think they were here already."

The other woman pressed a hand to her chest. "Why in the world would I do such a thing?" She delivered the words with enough sass that Ruby knew her suspicion was correct.

She pointed at her seneschal. "You require watching, troublemaker." She thought she'd managed to hide the surge of inappropriate anger that had run through her at the realization that Tirina was playing with her, but Keshalla's hand on her shoulder was her first clue that she hadn't. The hard squeeze she received from that hand was the other.

Her mentor announced, "That means you have the rest of the day available for training. Let's get to it."

As Keshalla led her away, she heard Idryll ask Tirina, "Is there a dictionary in this place? I need to look up a word."

CHAPTER SEVENTEEN

Ruby slashed and dodged as if her life depended on it, weaving her single sword in complex patterns to deflect her teacher's double-sword attacks. The huge room offered abundant space to maneuver, and the light spilling in the windows warmed it, causing her to freely sweat as she fought.

After a particularly demanding series of blocks, she asked, "Are you trying to kill me?"

Keshalla's neutral expression provided no clue as to her intentions. "If you can't defend yourself, do you deserve to live?"

Ruby stepped in and gave a mighty swing, gripping the sword hilt in both her hands. It blasted through her opponent's first effort to deflect it, but the other woman spun nimbly away, the move looking more like a dance than combat. The spin finished with a blade whistling in at Ruby's head. She backpedaled only far enough to avoid it, then tried to slide in behind the swing. Keshalla's other sword stabbed underneath, and she halted her advance and blocked it.

Her teacher circled, booted feet crossing over the top of one another as she calmly moved slightly inside the range of Ruby's reach. Her mentor gently but solidly deflected every strike she sent out. It felt very much like the other woman was playing with her.

Ruby's ire rose, and she snarled, "Don't mock me." Her left arm started to ache, and pain radiated through her head as the inhabitants of her sword acted to hold the artifact in check.

Keshalla only smiled and replied, "Do you feel mocked? Then do better."

Ruby burst into motion, charging and slashing, but her teacher calmly retreated, easily picking off the blows. She managed to sneak a kick through that caught Keshalla in the stomach and knocked her back a few steps, but the expression on the other woman's face never changed. It made her madder, and she strengthened her grip in preparation for the next attack.

Keshalla stepped backward and raised her swords, crossing them defensively. "Hold. We're finished."

Ruby growled, "Afraid you're going to lose?"

Keshalla shook her head. "Afraid you'll lose control. Check yourself." It was a phrase she'd used often during training, admonishing her student to examine her footwork, her body positioning, or the choices she was making. Ruby reacted instinctively to it, freezing in place and looking down at her feet. She realized an instant later, though, that the command was about her mental status, not her physical one.

With a murmured, "Thanks for being there, you two," she sheathed the sword in a smooth movement and sat, crossing her legs and closing her eyes. "I see what you mean."

Leather rustled as Keshalla matched her position. "You're still carrying the energy from your last fight." Ruby had told her about the battle on the way to the castle, both the good and the bad. "You need to let that go. I thought maybe we could burn it out of you with exercise, but it seems to go deeper than that."

Ruby nodded. "It's like it's part of my bones. The pressure from the artifact is greater than ever before and never goes away."

Keshalla asked, "Is it a real threat, or are you afraid of it?"

Ruby opened her mouth to reply that of course, it was a real threat, then she shut it again. *Is it? We were in a unique situation when it spilled out of me. Outnumbered, and without the support of Tyrsh and Shalia, since I was using my sword hand to maintain my shield spells.* She shook her head. "You know, you might be right. It could be more fear than threat."

Her mentor nodded. "So, how do we minimize the threat and thus reduce the fear?"

"I need to be able to cast with the sword."

Keshalla made a *swooshing* sound as she rose to her feet, and Ruby opened her eyes to see the other woman extending a hand to her. "Then let's do that."

By the time their training concluded an hour later, Ruby had it down. She had learned to open her mind only a little, to allow Tyrsh and Shalia to help her against the artifact. The small temporary pin she'd attached to the sword both helped to keep her focused and allowed her to project her power out of it like the Atlantean in her head had said it would.

She practiced attacks and defenses, and by the end of the session was confident she could use the strategy at will. It would still take some time to integrate it into her fighting style fully and to learn to trust that it would always be there when she called for it. *Once I do, watch out. I'm going to be wicked awesome.* It was with a feeling of satisfaction that she said, "Okay. We're good. I've got it. Now, let's get something to eat. Then I need a rest. Gotta play *Mirra* tomorrow, after all."

Keshalla laughed. "Let's hope the petitioners don't regret having asked you to help."

"Since Idryll's not here, I'll supply her answer: how could they not regret it? They'll have to deal with me."

A few minutes before noon on the following day, Ruby sat in an overly fancy chair in the audience chamber. It wasn't quite a throne, and the raised platform it rested upon wasn't quite a dais but inspired those ideas. She had dressed in her formal leathers, with the golden sash that served as the *Mirra's* "official business" signifier on top.

The night before, they'd toured more of the castle, and she'd seen paintings of the previous leaders wearing the item over gowns, over armor, and in one case, over a bare chest. Something involving an aquatic competition had resulted in that particular moment. *Here's hoping nothing from my time of service warrants a painting to immortalize it.*

The doors at the far end of the chamber opened, and a pair of male Mist Elves entered. Both were young, maybe in their twenties, and were slightly built. One had brown hair and the other red, but otherwise, they could've been brothers. The scowls they threw at each other as they walked toward her added to that impression.

They stopped at the appointed place, and Tirina announced, "Bern and Etone have requested an audience to request a boon and resolve a dispute."

Ruby frowned. "A boon and a dispute, you say?"

The other woman lifted an eyebrow, and a small smile twitched at the corners of her mouth. *She misinformed me on purpose yesterday. She really is a troublemaker. I like her.* "Yes, *Mirra.* I'm sure that won't prove too challenging."

Ruby matched the raised eyebrow. "I'm sure." She turned her head to the men and asked, "So, what's the deal?"

They both started talking at once. Instead of one surrendering the field to the other to explain, they both continued to speak. Ruby raised her hand. "Okay, stop. Redhead, speak. You," she pointed at Bern, "Silence."

From where she stood behind the chair, Idryll leaned over and whispered, "You're very imperial now that you're in charge."

Ruby didn't reply. The shapeshifter had the advantage because as *Mirra,* Ruby was on stage in any public setting. Etone explained, "I ask permission to leave the village and travel through Oriceran. We have been removed from the larger society so long and have lost the opportunity to gain so much knowledge. I wish to collect it and record it for our benefit."

Ruby asked, "Are you a mystic?" He didn't *look* like a mystic. Maybe he was a mystic in training?

He shook his head. "I'm a student, *Mirra*."

Ruby's glance landed on Keshalla, who stood quietly on one side of the room, ready to intervene should there be trouble. Ruby's sword was right behind her chair, against the same possibility. Her mentor rolled her eyes but nodded. Ruby said, "Okay, you're a student, and you want to visit other places on Oriceran so you can add your observations to the collective knowledge. So far, so good." She looked at the other one and ordered, "Bern, tell me your version."

The first speaker pressed his lips together, clearly irritated at her shift of attention. The other said, "Thank you, *Mirra*. The issue is that I want to do the same thing. In fact, it was my idea."

Etone interrupted, "No, it was *my* idea."

Brown Hair replied, "It was not, and you know it. I shared it with you during class, and—"

Ruby clapped her hands together and ordered, "Shut it, both of you." As they subsided into silence, Tirina caught her eye. "Yes?"

"It is customary for the *Mirra* to consider the question before ruling. In the past, some have done so for an hour, others for as much as a day."

Ruby nodded. "Excellent idea." She scowled at the petitioners. "You two, come back tomorrow. Unless you have actual evidence to present as to who came up with the idea first, other than your own competing opinions?" They both shook their heads reluctantly, and she nodded. "So, go."

When they left the room, Ruby said, "Thank you for the advice. Got any more?"

"Seek the wisdom of those who have preceded you."

She stood. "Exactly what I was thinking. First lunch, then a chat with the dead."

CHAPTER EIGHTEEN

Ruby sat in the chair as the door closed behind her and said, "Mintel, could I speak with you?"

The heavyset and mirthful ex-*Mirra* appeared before her, a smile on his face. A chair materialized beside him, and he lowered himself into it, perfectly at eye level with her. "So, to what do I owe the pleasure of this conversation?"

Ruby asked, "Are you bored?"

He looked surprised by the question. "No, not at all. I do not exist as such in between summonings, so no time has passed for me since we last spoke. I can see, though, that your clothes are changed, and your hair is a little different, so I presume time has passed for you."

She nodded. "It has, and to answer your first question, I've come to seek your advice."

He laughed. "Excellent. I've always loved giving advice. I'm sure that's recorded somewhere in the mystics' vast library."

"You know about the library?"

He shook his head. "Not as such. I assume it exists, knowing the mystics."

Ruby grinned. "It does, indeed. It's gorgeous. The archivist is a woman not to mess with." Her voice turned serious. "Petitioners have come to ask whether they can reengage with Oriceran. On a limited basis, as there's only a pair of them. I wanted to know for sure what happened during your time to convince you to pull away. After you, we maintained the policy because of Rhazdon, but I don't think she's a substantial concern anymore, at least not to these two."

He frowned and crossed his arms. "It was nothing I can put into specifics. It was a feeling, but no, more than that. A conviction. A *certainty*. I knew things would go horribly for us if we remained connected to the rest of the civilizations on this planet."

"Did any evidence come to light during your time that suggested you were correct?"

He chuckled. "No, nothing specific. Believe me; I was constantly looking for something that would bear out my decision."

She nodded in understanding. "You believe that certainty came to you through the magic inherent in the *venamisha*?"

He shrugged. "That's my best explanation. I mean, it's possible I'm psychic, or it might be that it deluded me. But I was convinced, and remain convinced, that it was the correct thing to do."

Ruby sighed. "The magic isn't giving me any particular guidance. At least none that I can detect."

"Perhaps that is, in itself, your answer."

She shook her head, more in confusion than denial. "I'm really sort of a science-y person. I like facts. Evidence. Predictability."

He laughed expansively. "Boy, are *you* in the wrong job."

"Right? The petitioners in question both have different stories, directly opposite ones, of course, with absolutely nothing to support either of them."

"This is why leading people is hard. *Things* behave in a certain way and generally continue to behave in that way, barring major issues. People, though, can't be counted on to act consistently from minute to minute, much less over a longer timeframe. They ebb and flow like the tides."

"That's very poetic."

He smiled. "I've always enjoyed words."

"A friend advised me that I should be kind when I can be, hard when I have to be, and fair as often as possible. Would you say that's true?"

He nodded. "Except be careful not to overdo the fair part because you'll want to. It's the easiest path, mentally. Sometimes the right decision isn't the fair one, and you always have to be open to that possibility. It's one of the least pleasant parts of the gig."

The way his face had fallen into a neutral expression and the slight sadness in his voice suggested he might have had occasion to experience that firsthand. She said, "That makes a lot of sense. Do you ever regret it?"

"Being *Mirra*?"

"Yeah. It seems like it must've been a huge burden for everyone who came before me."

A chuckle escaped him. "Oh, don't worry, I'm sure it will be a burden for you, too. No, I don't regret it. It was an awesome responsibility, and I did the best I could to uphold it. I succeeded sometimes, failed others, and wound up not making a difference at all more often than I would've liked. On the whole, the good outweighs the bad. And I continue to believe that we aren't chosen at random."

Ruby nodded. "Okay. I think I have some useful perspective now. Thank you so much."

He grinned. "Any time. Literally. Because I'm always here." He faded on another laugh, and she shook her head. *At least I don't have to worry about being the goofiest of the past Mirra since that position is already taken.*

The next day, right before noon, the scene from the day before played out again. The pair walked down the aisle, scowling and occasionally exchanging hissed words. When they reached the end, Tirina announced them. Ruby said, "So, you two. Do you still wish to petition me for a solution to your dispute?"

They both nodded and replied, "I do."

"Understanding that my word is binding?" They both repeated their answer, though each seemed a bit less confident about it. "Very well. Here's the deal. You have conditional permission to go out into Oriceran."

Both of them brightened, and the redhead said, "Thank you, *Mirra.*"

Ruby laughed. "That might be a little premature. Here are the conditions. First, you will present to me a list of the towns you intend to visit. They must be an even number, and you must plan to spend the same amount of time in each of them. After each two, you'll portal back here and supply a report to Tirina on your experiences. If she finds that things are progressing properly, we will authorize the next pair of locations."

They nodded. Probably, they'd jumped to the conclusion she was sending each of them to separate places, which would make the next part rather difficult for them. She ensured her expression remained neutral as she said, "You will be traveling together."

She paused, expecting an outburst, but all she got was stark looks. *Good, maybe if you can learn, you'll both survive this with your sanity intact.* "In each town, one of you will play the role of scholar. The other will be the scholar's mute servant, there to take notes and assist. Emphasis on the *mute* part."

They both broke out in objections, and she raised her hand. "Shut it, both of you. Etone, speak. Bern, pretend you're the mute servant."

The redhead replied, "Surely you're kidding, *Mirra.* What possible reason do you have for this decision?"

She shrugged. "It's equitable. Each of you will spend the same amount of time as a servant and scholar. Each of you will receive the same information firsthand, so you won't have to worry about the other party not sharing. Ultimately, you each get what you want, to experience Oriceran and learn about it. When all is said and done, you may find that you would prefer to write complementary records rather than duplicate ones, but that will be up to you."

The annoyance didn't leave his face, but a sense of thoughtfulness joined it. "Now, you pretend you're the one unable to speak."

She turned her head to the other, who said, "I don't think that's fair. You're asking us to put up with a lot when you could send us to separate places."

"It might not be fair, but it does ensure equality. Since neither of you can prove that the idea was yours, that's the best I can do. Besides, this way, you'll have the opportunity to share perspectives on what you've seen. In private, of course. That should make the experience more productive for both of you."

They looked about to argue, but Tirina raised her voice and announced, "The *Mirra* has ruled. You will inform me of your plans within a day. Off with you."

They all watched the duo walk down the long carpet and out the door at the far end. Their manner toward one another had distinctly changed from when they'd entered. Idryll observed, "Can't be as bad as being stuck with you."

Ruby rolled her eyes. "Predictable."

Keshalla laughed and approached her position. "I think it was a great solution."

"Ah, but you believe pain should accompany all learning."

"Apparently I've taught you that well. My work here progresses nicely."

Ruby snorted, then addressed Tirina. "What do you think?"

The woman smiled. "I think they got exactly what they deserved. Each other. By the end of this, they'll be fast friends, or they'll be petitioning to be allowed to fight to the death."

Idryll replied, "I'd watch that. They don't look particularly martial. There would probably be a lot of amusing flailing around and slapping."

Ruby laughed. "Well, then, I'd say this one's a win. Now I have to get back to Earth. Responsibilities await there, too." It didn't escape her attention that helping the duo with their problem had allowed her to get a little distance from hers, which seemed less threatening and less scary because of it. *I'm a very lucky person, both in the challenges I face and the people I face them with. I need to remember that more often.*

CHAPTER NINETEEN

Ruby's phone rang, startling her. Most of the people she communicated with used text or their shared comms. She answered it. "Hello?"

Shiannor's voice came from the other end, with the sound of Grinding Axes behind him. She knew that's where he was because she recognized Jastrum in the background, shouting at someone. She'd kept the elf's involvement with the Hat's gang secret, and as near as she could tell, he hadn't continued as part of the group after the events at the warehouse. *Which makes sense. He's not Drow, so he's probably not welcome.* She hoped he'd broken up with the girl who'd led him into the organization. He said, "Domick needs to talk to you."

She frowned but replied, "Okay."

The phone rustled as he handed it over, and the dwarven bartender's voice came over the line. "A friend of yours from here in the bar is trying to reach you. Says it's urgent."

It could only be Grentham. She hadn't trusted him with

her contact information directly, fearing what he might have an infomancer do if he had her direct line. Instead, she'd suggested he use the bartenders as a relay since they knew how to get in touch with Liam, and Liam had her number. The elf being in the bar at the right time was a lucky coincidence. She replied, "Okay. Tell him I'll be at the meeting spot in fifteen."

She instinctively started to create a portal to the bunker, then laughed at herself. "Idiot. Grentham needs Ruby Achera, not Magic City's defender. Honestly, I don't know how Diana Prince managed the whole secret identity thing. She had more clothes and glasses, but that's about it."

Ruby slipped on her shield pendant, stuffed a couple of lightning grenade discs into her pockets as an emergency backup, and patted her shoulders to make sure her capsules were in place. Confident that she was ready to go, she opened a portal from her surface bedroom to an alley behind The Underground casino.

Grentham was waiting when she stepped out, pacing and looking concerned. He said, "I received word from someone who works for Sloane on occasion. They're going after my partner. It's not Worldspan, but I could still use your help since you have so much experience with illusion and disguise."

She nodded. "This will set us at even."

"Done. As soon as we get in, block the windows." He opened a portal, and Ruby stepped through it into a hospital room. She immediately replicated the room in the windows so no one would notice them unless they'd been looking at that exact second. An elf sitting in a chair jerked up, and a dwarf leaning against the door drew a pistol, but Grentham said, "It's me. Hold."

The man on the bed, obviously Jared Trenton, asked, "They're coming?"

Grentham nodded. "You're going. Don't even try to argue." He opened another portal and helped his partner out of bed. Ruby assisted, and together they took him through into a warehouse of some kind, filled with magicals engaged in various tasks. Grentham called for help immediately, and several of them came over with a wheelchair to take Jared off their hands. "We've already got a bed set up for you. You'll be fine."

His partner replied, "Assuming we didn't rip something important inside of me."

Grentham sighed. "Quit worrying. You're not that fragile." He gestured for Ruby to follow as he stepped back through the portal. His guards were standing around, looking confused, and he sent them on to the warehouse.

He turned to her. "Willing to help me turn the tables on that wench?"

Ruby nodded. "Figured that was part of the deal."

"I like the way you think. I'll get in the bed, and you can make me look like Jared. Disguise yourself as the elf, throw up an illusion of the other dwarf, and we'll wait for whoever's going to show up." He snapped his fingers. "Hang on a sec. I need to tell the two outside to fall for whatever distraction they try. Because they will."

"Think she'll have backup?"

He shrugged. "Maybe."

She nodded. "Okay, when she gets here, we portal her and us to a neutral location. We can call the PDA and the sheriff and have them ready to roll on any friends she brings."

Grentham grinned. "Excellent plan. Not sure it's the PDA's jurisdiction, but what the hell. The more, the merrier." He went out and talked to his people, then came back in and leapt up to the bed. Ruby carefully didn't smile at the sight.

She cast the illusions, making him look like Jared, longer legs that didn't exist appearing to push up the covers. She transformed herself into the elf and added the dwarf at the door. Then she sat in the chair and flicked open the magazine, releasing the illusion covering the windows to show the room as it now was.

Grentham-Jared grinned, and she could still see some of the dwarf's attitude in the human features that disguised him. "I can't wait to see the look on her face."

***

Vicki Thompson was not a fan of the plan her boss had come up with. Her displeasure expressed itself in a heavier stride than usual, almost a stomp, as she and two of her most trusted subordinates marched toward the hospital entrance. Several teams were in backup positions, ready to take out the target should he use any of the exits.

She was fully aware that there would be magicals standing guard over the human owner of Aces Security. The anti-magic emitter in her pocket was bulky enough that its presence was notable, but she doubted anyone would think twice about it if they noticed it at all. She didn't want her quarry portaled away before she could kill him.

Her information said two guards were outside the room and one inside with the patient, all magicals. With the emitter to level the playing field, she was confident she could take out everyone inside the room in seconds with her silenced pistol, retrieve the device, and leave without being detected.

They entered and headed for the elevator, planning to ride to one level under the target's room. A distraction on the floor below would likely peel away one of the guards. Vicki's other companion would create a second diversion after she'd found a secure hiding spot, hopefully drawing the other one away. If it failed, she'd force the remaining guard into the room and shoot him, too.

Her first helper got out and immediately headed for the janitorial closet to start a fire. Scimitar had secured the blueprints for the hospital, and she trusted that the info-mancer had the latest information. They arrived at the target's floor, and she got into position in a convenient lounge off the main corridor. When the alarm went off on the floor below, one of the guards ran off as expected.

The other one hesitated, seeming about to follow. Her escort on this level pulled the fire alarm and yelled, "Fire, come help, someone's hurt." The second guard ran to assist, and Vicki made her way to the door, put one hand on the handle and the other on the anti-magic emitter, and pushed her way in. The emitter was active in seconds, rolling on the floor between the bed and the elf in the chair.

Vicki's pistol was halfway out of its holster when the

image in front of her wavered, and the elf became a different elf, a woman instead of a man, one she thought she recognized from somewhere. The human in the bed transformed into the dwarf she loathed, and he was already in motion toward her. She got the gun the rest of the way out, but not before Grentham reached her and locked his hands on her arm, preventing her from bringing it to bear.

The woman in the chair stood calmly, grabbed the emitter, and hurled it out the window with a loud *crash*. *Damn. That possibility didn't even occur to me. Idiot.* She rammed her knee into the dwarf's stomach, but he took the blow and stubbornly refused to let go of her arm. She started to feel like she might be in trouble, and when the elf in front of her motioned elaborately, she knew she was.

The unreal sensation of traveling through a portal, which she'd most recently enjoyed thanks to the bastard gripping her gun hand, nauseated her again as he drove her through the one the elf had created. Grentham pushed her away, and a magic fist slapped the weapon from her grasp. The elf came through, and the rift closed behind her.

Grentham didn't pursue her as she stepped away, only said, "Not cool, trying to kill a hospitalized man."

Vicki nodded. She gazed around, taking in the abandoned building. It looked like it had probably been a garage once upon a time, now forgotten. "I won't say there's not a little personal in it, but mostly it was business. The boss wanted it. Now killing you, that would have been way more personal."

The elf woman asked, "Who is your boss?"

She closed her lips, but the dwarf laughed. "Sloane, of course."

The elf shrugged. "Guess you were right. Anyway, the sheriff is arresting your backup teams, so you can consider this a loss for your side."

Vicki said, "So what now? You take me in?"

Grentham shook his head. "Things between us can't end like that. We have too much history. I beat the hell out of you. *Then* we take you in."

She laughed. "As if I have any chance against you with your magic. I think I'll surrender to her instead. She seems upstanding. Unlike you."

The elf replied, "Or you. I wouldn't get too haughty, given what you tried to do a couple of minutes ago."

Grentham said, "I'll commit to not using my magic. We'll go toe-to-toe. You get to kill me if you can, but I'll stop before you're dead so the upstanding one can hand you over to the authorities."

Vicky turned to the elf. "You're good with that?"

She shrugged. "I'm only here as a helper. It's his call."

She took off her jacket and smiled at the dwarf who'd killed her partner. "Well, if I'm going to jail regardless, seems like causing you some serious pain first is the more enjoyable way to go."

CHAPTER TWENTY

Grentham had brought his axes, and Thompson pulled out a baton and flicked it to full extension. The wench observed, "Kind of unfair already, don't you think?"

He shrugged. "You have a longer reach. I have two weapons. Seems okay to me."

She shook her head. "The difference is that mine's only impact. Yours can cut. I'm supposed to trust that you're not going to kill me in a single pass?"

Grentham sighed. "I could say I'm good enough to avoid it, but I doubt you'll believe me."

Achera solved the problem. "I'll coat his blades with force magic so they don't cut. I do it all the time in training. It's one of the first pieces of magic we learn."

Thompson replied, "I can't trust him, but I'm supposed to trust you?"

The elf woman shrugged. "Doesn't matter to me. I get what I want, no matter how this ends. If one of you winds up making a trip to the hospital first, that's your choice. If you'd like me to take you in right now, I will."

The look on her face suggested she was seriously considering it. He would've preferred to think it was because she was afraid of him, but he doubted that was true. Thompson wasn't the type to be scared of anything. She was simply calculating what would give her the most advantage, possibly balancing it against what would give her the most pleasure.

At least, that's what he was counting on. He wouldn't feel right handing her over without some sort of punishment and might have to grab her and spirit her away from Achera if she chose that option. *I never promised to play by her rules, and like she said, we're even now.*

Thompson nodded. "Okay. I don't trust him, but I think I can trust you."

Grentham grinned. "Whenever you're ready." His opponent smiled, then made a show of stretching, warming up her muscles with arm circles and quick jogs. After half a minute, he was sure she was doing it to be irritating. He said sweetly, "I have no plans for the day, so you know, take whatever time you need."

She stopped with a scowl and stepped back into a guard stance with the weapon held angled in front of her. "Bring it, Shorty."

He rolled his eyes. "Inventive. I hope you fight better than you trash talk." He faked a rush, and she flinched. With a laugh, he shook his head and started the circle. "If you're that nervous already, things aren't going to go well for you."

"You talk big for someone who's gotten his ass kicked repeatedly and publicly." She darted forward and snapped the baton out at his face. He crossed his offhand ax in front of him to knock it aside, and she went with the block, going low and spinning to slash the weapon at his ankles. He hopped backward to avoid it, letting it pass underneath him, and stopped the instinctive reflex to throw his ax while she was down.

That works when it's sharp. She's probably got body armor under there like Smith did, so unless I get the perfect hit, I won't do more than bruise her. With a static target, he could easily control what part of the ax would hit. But with her in motion, a step forward or back would change that calculus and leave him one weapon down without causing her any notable damage. *All that assumes she's not quick enough to block it, which she might be.*

She rose and stalked toward him, swiping the baton every time he tried to take a step forward. *Okay, so that's how you're going to play it. I have an answer for that.* He charged in and intercepted her weapon with his left-hand ax, then swung the other at her ribs.

He expected her to block down, had prepared a counter for that move, but she didn't. The ax smashed into her side, and she grunted at the impact. That she failed to crumple over with shattered ribs confirmed she was wearing protection underneath her clothes. *Dammit. Those things must be almost skintight to not show through their shirts.*

Her left fist crashed into his cheek with unexpected force, and he stepped back, shaking his head and moving his mouth to be sure that she hadn't broken anything. He spat out blood onto the dirty floor of the abandoned building. "Nice one. You failed to mention the armor you're wearing."

Thompson laughed. "Pretty sure you have some protective gear on, too. I figured you expected that. Or did I misjudge your insight?"

He shook his head. "No, I knew. Sloane gets you guys good stuff."

His opponent shrugged. "Had you and your partner been at all competent, she probably would've gotten the same for you."

He started in with a sudden shout, hoping to startle her, and chopped both axes down from overhead. She whipped the baton across at chest level to intercept them, and he snapped out a kick at her knee. She twisted, taking it on the side of the joint rather than allowing him to break it, and went down onto that leg. Despite enough pain to make her snarl in anger, she maintained control of his axes. He was fine with that arrangement and kicked again, striking her on the other shin.

She pushed off and rolled aside, coming up hobbled. He advanced, and she circled, keeping the wounded leg away from him. He remarked happily, "Won't be long now."

She shook her head and gestured at her mostly unharmed leg. "I have another one."

He laughed. "You're tough as steel."

She nodded. "And you're as smart as the stuff."

He saw an opening but didn't take it. *Could be a trap, have to see if she does it again.* "You know, I probably could've liked you if you weren't working for such a wench."

Her voice sounded regretful. "Sometimes our leaders disappoint us. For a while there, though, I thought she'd succeed." She laughed. "Well, she certainly succeeded in screwing up your life, so that's something."

Her steps had become predictable, and he smiled. "And yours, if you think about it." He threw the ax, and it slammed into her good knee, fracturing or breaking the kneecap and demolishing the joint underneath. She fell with a cry, and he advanced, ready to bash her skull in. A wall of force stopped him, and Achera said, "Now, now. Remember the deal."

Grentham sighed and pulled his righteous desire to see his foe's brains on the floor back from the edge. "Right. She's yours." He looked down at the writhing woman. "If you get the chance to talk to your boss, let her know my partner and I are coming after her next."

A couple of hours later, Ruby watched through the window of the interrogation cell as Sheriff Alejo exchanged words with Vicki Thompson. They'd dosed the prisoner with pain medication, so whatever she said wouldn't be admissible in court. Ruby wasn't worried about that at the moment, and neither was the sheriff. Alejo, seated across a metal table from Thompson, asked, "So, what's your boss up to?"

The other woman was almost giddy and laughed loudly at the question. "So much stuff. Wheels within wheels. *Big* stuff. Magic City will be her playground, she says."

Alejo sighed. "Any chance you could be a little less crazy and a little more specific?"

Thompson shook her head. "Nope. But hey, this pain medication is groovy. Thanks for that."

"Tell me this, then. How do you think Grentham beat you?"

She scowled. "Scimitar. Bastard." Then her face went canny as if she was trying to be deceptive. "I mean, he probably figured we'd try for his partner and decided to wait it out. Not like he had anything else to do, given the wreckage of his business." She laughed again.

Alejo rose. "Sure, I bet that's it. Can I get you something?"

"I'd take a cheeseburger."

Alejo chuckled. "Yeah, sure. I'll grab you a cup of coffee instead." She exited the room and came to where Ruby was standing.

Ruby asked, "Scimitar?"

The other woman shrugged. "No idea. I imagine it's important. Maybe you can ask Grentham about it."

"Makes sense. I'll let you know what I find out."

CHAPTER TWENTY-ONE

Ruby had indeed asked Grentham about Scimitar, and he'd shared that she was an infomancer he'd worked with once upon a time. The dwarf had seemed reluctant to say more and had kind of bristled at the mention of her name, so she'd let it drop.

She hadn't let it drop far. Her next stop was Demetrius's room. She sat on his lap, facing him and blocking his view of his screens. "You adore me, right?"

He leaned back and laughed. "Of course I do. Why do you ask?"

She grinned. "Just checking. In my experience, when you adore someone, you're willing to do things for them. Do you concur with that statement?"

He lifted an eyebrow. "Well, there are things, and there are *things*. Some of which are far more fun than others. Somehow, though, I don't think you're thinking of the same things I'm thinking of."

She nodded. "I need to chat with an infomancer."

"I'm an infomancer."

Ruby slapped him on the chest and laughed. "Not you, goof. Someone named Scimitar. Have you ever heard of her?"

He shrugged. "I've heard a lot of names, and that's one of them. It's more like I'm aware of her than I know of her. Assuming it's a her."

Ruby climbed off his lap. "I need to have a chat with her, and I'd prefer to do it on our terms rather than hers."

She hopped over to the bed and fell on it with a sigh. He spun the chair to look at her. "What's her role in this particular play?"

Ruby propped herself up on her elbows. "She's worked with Grentham. She's currently working for Julianna Sloane, the wife of the late and unlamented Gabriel 'The Nightmare' Sloane. The widow has a beef with Magic City and plans to do something about it."

He frowned. "You came by this flood of interesting information how?"

She let herself fall back on the bed. "Long story, but I helped Grentham with a thing, and it led to this."

Demetrius shook his head. "It's a weird life you lead, Ruby Achera."

Stranger than you know. "Yeah. I get that. Aren't you lucky I allow you to be a part of it?"

He laughed. "Yep. Feeling totally lucky right now."

"So, will you help me?"

With a chuckle, he asked, "What's in it for me?"

With a groan, she pushed herself up to a sitting position. "Besides my everlasting respect and affection?"

"Besides that."

"A date. A real one, again. I'll do all the planning. You can come along and be my kept man."

He grinned. "Perfect. Done. Give me fifteen minutes to wrap up what I'm working on here. In the meantime, go over to the top drawer of the dresser, pull out the VR rig, and get it hooked up."

He'd shown her the equipment before, although they hadn't had occasion to use it. By the time he'd closed the final window on his work, she was seated in a comfortable chair beside him, with the virtual reality goggles perched on the top of her head. She asked, "So, this will allow me to experience it like you do, right?"

He lifted his hand and waggled it. "Sort of. I receive more sensory information than you'll have through the headset. You'll have sight and sound, but I get taste, touch, and all sorts of other fun experiences."

"Infomancy is so weird." He'd explained that for him, it was like navigating a video game. The style changed from time to time, either because he willed it so or because the systems he was entering had preferences. It sounded like fun, but she hadn't had the opportunity to ride along on anything serious, had only seen what he called the landing construct on his screens. She asked, "Is it the same for all infomancers?"

"Not really. We all experience things differently. No one's sure if it's because our magic is different, or because our personalities are, or what. Some people see the virtual world inside the computers as blocks of code, like in *The Matrix*. Others see it as the real world, with all the appropriate rules and so forth."

"You see it as a combination of those, right? You can mess with the rules a little, but the world has a theme to it."

Demetrius nodded. "Sometimes, when I'm tired or really into a new video game, I can't control the surroundings. They generally wind up being either *Minecraft*, which I used to play a lot or whatever game I'm into at the moment. Today will be fantasy or post-apocalypse."

She pulled the goggles down over her eyes. "You don't know which?"

He shrugged. "I could force one or the other, but the easier thing to do is leave both options open. Then see where we wind up when we try to make contact with Scimitar's systems."

The screen lit up, and they were suddenly in a garden, with flowing fountains and rock walls, hedges and flowers, and buzzing insects. She said, "*Skyrim*, right?"

"Kind of. A combo of that and *Witcher 3*. I rarely get one game anymore, more of a mashup of the things I like best from a certain genre."

Ruby replied, "You're totally weird, you know that?"

"Yeah. I do. Part of my charm. Okay, let's go looking for our enigmatic infomancer."

Without transition, they were flying, the ground speeding by below in a greenish blur. They wove unpredictably and changed direction, seemingly at random. Ruby asked, "What is this?"

He replied, "We're in the magical version of the Internet. Each turn is a different system we're passing through on our search for Scimitar."

"How will you know when we've got a lead?"

He gestured ahead. "It's a fantasy game, so we look for

something you would typically follow inside that kind of story. Like that will-o'-the-wisp over there."

She spotted the thing he was talking about, a small pale blue light pulsing in front of them. "I thought you weren't supposed to trust will-o'-the-wisps."

"Different stories, different rules. In my world, they're okay."

"What if we're actually in Scimitar's world, and she's making it seem like it's yours?"

He laughed. "What if we're actually in my world, and she *thinks* we're in her world and that she's tricking us?"

Ruby sighed. "You suck."

"I know. Trust me. The wisp is our friend."

They flew through the sky for several minutes, following the glowing light that always seemed on the verge of escaping from them. Finally, a castle came into view on top of the hill. It had a vague resemblance to the image at the start of Disney films, but as if drawn by a modern artist. It was jagged, bold colored, the very opposite of sinuous in most respects. She said, "What the hell?"

Demetrius shrugged. "Often, infomancer handles are symbolic. Hers is a curved blade, so you'd think she'd want curves, but this seems to represent the blade part well. It also suggests she's adept at playing with those who are looking for her since it's not what we'd expect."

"Fantastic."

"Okay, hang on. By now she knows we're seeking her. If she's willing to meet, things will probably change suddenly. If she's not, the change will still happen suddenly, but in a much more violent way."

"Can you actually get hurt in here?"

The virtual version of him shook his head. "We're not jacked in like in *The Matrix*. I might get a little magical feedback, but nothing that'll do major damage. Unless you have epilepsy, you shouldn't be at any risk either."

She asked, "What about viruses and stuff?"

"I have the best protections money and code customization can provide. Don't worry." In an instant, the sky vanished, the castle vanished, and the wisp vanished. Her stomach tried to keep moving forward, even though her virtual body was suddenly seated in a large and overly padded chair. Demetrius was in another one beside her. Across from them, in a black leather chair that was even bigger than theirs, sat a woman.

Her features were utterly average, as was her hair. She looked like a construct that wasn't quite at full resolution. When she spoke, her synthesized voice added to that feeling, as did the way her avatar's lips didn't perfectly sync with the words. "What do you want?"

Demetrius said, "My companion was looking for you."

The expressionless gaze turned to her. "And?"

Ruby replied, "A mutual friend gave me your name. Grentham. He says you still owe him, by the way."

A chuckle emanated from the other figure, although the mouth didn't move to produce it. "Yes, he would. Again, what do you want?"

"I'm interested in protecting Magic City from danger. One of Julianna Sloane's people suggested there's something big coming up but wouldn't give us any more information. I thought you might have some."

The other woman's expression changed to a scowl. "And you assumed I'd give you this for free, right?"

Ruby shrugged. "If there's a cost, I would probably be willing to pay it. But it seems to me you might have some bad karma to work off, based on who you've been associating with."

Scimitar's frown deepened. "It wasn't voluntary. The Nightmare was okay, but his wife is worse, and I'm tired of being under her thumb. You're right. She is planning something big. I don't have the location yet, but she's asked me to pull all the information I can on the casinos in Magic City."

Ruby replied incredulously, "Do you think she intends to go after all of them?"

The figure in front of them shook her head. "Doubtful. I think she's looking for an opportunity. You never know, with her. Look at what her husband tried to accomplish."

Ruby remembered the trucks filled with explosives outside multiple casinos and shivered. "Right. Good reminder. Listen, can I count on you to let us know if you find out anything?"

The figure was immobile for several seconds, then finally, it lurched back into life. "Yes. Okay. Give me the means to drop information to you, and I will. You don't contact me, though. This is strictly one way. No one can see me as part of this."

"I understand. Sweetheart?"

Demetrius laughed. "Sending you an email address now. Toss anything in there, and we'll be alerted."

Scimitar said, "I hope you realize who you're going up against. This is the biggest of the big time."

Ruby nodded. "That's life in Magic City. The stakes are always high."

The other woman expelled a dark laugh. "Marketing slogans won't help you survive whatever Julianna has planned."

She replied, "Doesn't make it less true. Thanks for your help."

The world blurred like Scimitar had hurled out of the room, and suddenly they were back in Demetrius's starting room. He gave a loud sigh, and Ruby took off her VR rig to find him leaning back in his chair, stretching. She said, "That went about as well as could be expected."

He nodded. "Yeah. She seems okay."

She looked at her watch. "That didn't take long. Means I have an hour before I have to leave. Got any ideas on how to kill an hour?"

He laughed and moved over to the bed. "I bet I can think of something. Get over here."

CHAPTER TWENTY-TWO

When Thompson hadn't checked in at the designated time, Julianna had been concerned but not panicked. Several outcomes to the planned operation would have required her lieutenant to go to ground and stay that way for twenty-four hours. When one of her security team, a man named Stevens, requested to visit her, she knew something had gone wrong. She arranged herself on the edge of her couch and steeled herself for whatever news he would bring.

He entered the room almost reluctantly. He looked young to her but had the bearing of the military. It was visible in his stance, in his closely cropped hair, and in the way his hands clasped naturally behind his back when he greeted her.

Julianna nodded. "Out with it."

He replied, "The authorities have detained Ms. Thompson. By all indications, her operation was unsuccessful, as well."

Juliana appreciated the clarification. If they'd arrested

Thompson for murder, it would be much more difficult to arrange for her freedom. She said, "Get her released immediately."

He gave a slight head shake. "We've already looked into that option, ma'am, including contacting the lawyer you have on retainer. She's with the sheriff, not Ely PD. We have no leverage to apply, and standard procedure keeps her locked up without bail while the investigation continues."

"Do we know what went wrong?"

"We don't, unfortunately."

She nodded slowly, plans forming in her mind. "Okay. First thing to do is to dispatch one of our lawyers to her wherever they're holding her. They can get us some information, and we'll decide on our path forward from there. Have no doubt, I want her back. You're going to make that happen."

He straightened further and gave a sharp nod. "Yes, ma'am."

Julianna rose. "Go to it. Also, double my guard, and bolster our numbers with trusted people. This might be the first step in action against us. Finally, see that I'm not disturbed for the next two hours."

"Affirmative, ma'am." He backed out of her line of sight. She turned and headed for her bedroom, far less confident than the display she'd put on made her seem. *I really hoped I wouldn't have to do this. Ever.*

She angled into her walk-in closet and flicked on the light. A safe stood bolted to both the floor and the wall behind it. She pressed both of the buttons necessary to deactivate the security alarms that would go off when anyone touched the dial, then spun it to enter the five-number combination her husband had chosen at random and required her to memorize. With the final one entered, she was able to lift the heavy latch, and the door swung smoothly open.

The safe was smaller on the inside than it appeared on the outside, thanks to the protections built-in. The entire building could be on fire, and the papers inside the metal behemoth would survive, allegedly. She'd never needed to test it, fortunately. It held stacks of cash, her emergency run money. She had more squirreled away in various locations in the western part of the country, ready for her to access if circumstances required it.

On a shelf above that was a pistol, one her lieutenants had cleaned regularly, and that was always loaded. However, it was the metal container bolted to the top level that was her objective. It had five unlabeled buttons on the front, and she pressed them in the required sequence. That door released and swung aside, giving access to her false identities and a thick notebook. She left the former in the box and took the latter. Locking the safe again, she headed for her bed and threw herself on it.

She opened the notebook and smiled at the sight of her husband's cramped handwriting. *Late husband.* The realization still hit her anew at odd times. The entry she was looking for was on one of the most recently inked pages, inscribed there when a person Gabriel had helped at the early part of their career rose to a position of prominence.

Juliana didn't like having to call in favors from others. She didn't like that at all. Her husband had always warned her against negotiating from a weakened position, but she saw no other remaining options. She needed more firepower than she had at hand, and with her trusted lieutenants gone, could think of only one way to get it. Drawing a deep breath, she reached for her phone. She punched in the numbers that would begin the series of contacts that would hopefully result in an agreement to bring Magic City to heel once and for all.

Ruby sat at one end of an oval table with Morrigan and Idryll in the chairs to her right. To her left sat Cara, and across the table was Diana Sheen, leader of the aptly named Federal Agents of Magic. Even though Nylotte had warned that Diana's people didn't have the bandwidth to help, Ruby had reached out and gotten them to agree to spend a little time strategizing with her.

Cara asked, "So, do you think the attack is more likely to be on a casino that Worldspan Security is working in, or one they aren't?"

Morrigan interrupted her reply, saying, "My vote is one of the Worldspan ones. They're already there. All they have to do is throw open the doors and not act in defense."

Ruby shook her head. "That would make them look pretty bad, don't you think? After all this effort to get people to perceive them as the most competent company, it would be hideously off-brand for them not to do their job."

Diana chuckled. "And branding is everything in the casino world, right?"

Morrigan said, "You're not wrong. Okay, if we accept

it's most likely one of the other two, which will it be, Invention or The Underground?"

Ruby replied, "Well, they have experience with Invention. That might count for something."

Cara asked, "Is there a reason they can't hit both?"

The question took her momentarily aback. "I guess not. We should probably assume they're planning to attack both because we'll have plans in place to deal with it whether it's one, the other, or really both."

Diana said, "You have our apologies that we can't be there with you for this one. We'd all like to be." Cara nodded. "Unfortunately, our participation in the goings-on in Ely has ruffled some feathers in our command hierarchy. Until we smooth it over, we have to be a little more circumspect than usual."

Cara laughed. "You're the very poster child for discretion, Boss."

Diana flipped off her subordinate, causing everyone at the table to laugh. Idryll asked, "Is there anything we can do to help?"

Diana shook her head. "Not a thing. We'll make sure you have supplies, and if the timing works out, Deacon and Kayleigh can assist. No one ever knows what they're up to anyway, so they have some latitude."

"Including you?"

The agents' leader rolled her eyes. "Especially me. I'm usually the last to know about their antics. Fortunately, their work is so good that it's not an issue."

Ruby said, "So, we'll need to be aware of potential attacks on both the outside and the inside. Drones will help with the former, and maybe your people can assist my infomancer to hack the casinos' internal security."

Diana nodded, but Cara frowned. "I know technology is great, and you should totally use it, but you might want to find a way to get some human intel going inside and outside, too. If it's something big like your source suggests, they could have options in place to disable or evade ordinary surveillance measures."

Ruby replied, "Adding it to the list." Over the next half-hour, they came up with many more items to add to her to-do queue. When they'd run out of improvements to make, she whispered to Idryll, "Distract Cara and Morrigan," then headed toward Diana.

The shapeshifter loudly asked a random question about the agent's background, drawing Morrigan into the conversation by mentioning her depressing lack of martial training. Diana grinned at Ruby's approach. "Quite a companion you've got there."

Ruby nodded. "One-of-a-kind, no doubt. I'm not sure if that's fortunate or unfortunate, though. Depends on the day." She lowered her voice. "Listen, I wanted to say this one-on-one. We can cut off contact right now if that would help you all. You've given us so much, and I hate the idea that we're causing trouble for you."

Diana snorted derisively. "No way. We'll need to be more careful about what others find out. The day I let some scumbag politician in Washington tell me how to do my job is the day I hand in my resignation and become a freelance bounty hunter or something." She laughed unexpectedly. "Well, except for Bryant. But he's only *half* a scumbag politician, tops."

Ruby grinned. "I'd like to meet this mysterious boyfriend of yours. Idryll thinks he's imaginary."

Diana nodded. "Back at the beginning, he was around much more than he is now. Even then, though, no one knew much about him. I used to joke that his real name was Bryant Classified." She shook her head. "A lot of water under the bridge since then, that's for sure."

Ruby said, "Maybe when this is all over, we can have a picnic or something. Softball game, Agents versus, well, whatever we are."

Diana lifted an eyebrow. "Vigilantes?"

She shrugged. "You know, as a team name, it's not the worst thing ever." They laughed and went to rejoin the others. *Okay. Time to get to work knocking items off the list. No telling how long the bad guys will give us, but I'm sure it won't be as much time as we'd like to have.*

CHAPTER TWENTY-THREE

Ruby wasn't sure when they'd be ready to start watching over the casinos, but figured that if she was going to make good on her promise of a date with Demetrius, she needed to do it sooner rather than later. Fortunately, the Desert Ghosts had a party planned for that evening. She took a few minutes to polish up her new ARCH-1, which was delivered only a day before, then went up to her room to get dressed.

When she emerged, it was in a green dress she considered cute, high black boots she considered both sexy and practical, and her favorite leather jacket, the black one with a full-color picture of Dralen Bowie as Ziggy Stardust on the back. She knocked on Demetrius's door. "Come on, loser. Get a move on."

He opened it, and she lost control of her breathing for a moment. He was wearing black leather pants and biker boots, neither of which she'd ever seen him in, plus a white T-shirt and a black vest. She finally remembered how to breathe again. "Holy hell. You're hot."

He laughed. "Glad you think so."

Ruby shook her head. "Seriously. Why don't you dress like this all the time?"

"Leather is overly warm and not all that comfortable to work in."

"We need to go on more dates, then. Speaking of which, let's not be late, or Prex will give me annoying tasks to make up for it."

Her boyfriend offered, "Whatever they are, I'll help."

She chuckled. "Oh, you're already going to help. Part of my gig as a probational member is getting things set up for the party. It's just that if we don't get it done in time, I'll wind up having to do something stupid as penance instead of enjoying myself. With you looking like that, I am definitely not letting you hang out on your own around that bunch. Too many gorgeous, predatory women. And men, for that matter."

He replied, "I think I like the way jealousy looks on you."

A mock scowl covered her face. "Shut it and get downstairs."

They arrived in plenty of time to complete the preparatory tasks, then sat with the dwarven leader of the Desert Ghosts in folding chairs under a giant umbrella. It looked as if someone had stolen it from an island-themed bar. She remarked on it, and Prex explained, "Chain restaurant went out of business. We bought a lot of their stuff on the cheap."

Ruby lifted an eyebrow. "Bought it, you say?"

He grinned. "Well, most of it. Probably. I'm not saying a

few things didn't make it on the truck that they didn't strictly list in the exchange."

Ruby laughed, and Demetrius joined. She'd explained to him on the way over that while the Desert Ghosts weren't one hundred percent compliant with any particular set of laws, their good dramatically outweighed their bad, and she considered them at least allies and maybe family.

The night went by in a pleasant blur. Ruby made the rounds to introduce Demetrius as her boyfriend to the rest of the crew. They made many, many jokes at his expense and a few at hers. At first, he seemed nervous, not quite fitting in. She kept a strong grip on his arm, ensuring he knew she was there for him, and eventually, he loosened up and began to get into it.

By the time the clock ticked over to the next day, the party had settled into a gentle vibe, and she was able to isolate Prex from his people in the kitchen for a serious conversation. Demetrius leaned against a wall as the dwarf busied himself cutting up various Italian meats to put between huge slabs of bread he'd sliced from a fresh loaf. Ruby had never met the club's cooking staff, but they were without question excellent at what they did. The parties always had fantastic food, and they kept the refrigerator constantly stocked. She said, "Something big might be about to happen in Magic City."

He chuckled. "In the time before a casino blew up, I might've thought 'big' meant a robbery or something. How big are we talking?"

She shook her head. "I can't be sure. But some folks I trust suggested we might need more than electronic surveillance. I wondered if you could set up some patrols to ride around the casinos and make sure things are okay, as often as it's reasonable to do it. Plus, if you've got the people, maybe send some inside a couple of specific places to keep an extra eye on them."

He asked, "Which ones?"

"Invention and The Underground." She knew those names would increase his interest.

He set down his utensils and looked up at her. "Those are the two that Grentham still has contracts with. I'm guessing that's not a coincidence."

Ruby shook her head. "We think they're the most vulnerable right now. Not because of anything Grentham's doing, but because of the way the big picture has been playing out. It seems as if Aces has a target on their back, which might be enough of an incentive for someone to select one of their casinos."

He nodded. "We'll do it, but I want a promise from you. If you find something out that will help Grentham, you'll share it. I know you're not his biggest fan, and I completely understand why. But some things are bigger than feelings."

Ruby chuckled and offered him a smile. "Actually, you'll be shocked to learn that we have more than a truce and less than a partnership going on at the moment. He helped me with a thing, and I helped him with a thing. Anyway, I'm happy to share information with him. Feel free to pass on whatever you think needs passing on."

She frowned, then clarified, "I should mention that he only knows me as Ruby Achera, and I'd like to keep it that way. He's not as perceptive as you all."

Prex laughed. "Well, don't forget, we met you the other way around. Costume first."

Demetrius said, "That sounds like a story."

Prex grinned and put the final touches on the assembly of his snack. "Come on. I'll share it."

Ruby sighed and followed. "I'm definitely going to need a drink to deal with this."

The next day found them all sober, either from time or magic, and riding through town on the regular charity run. Demetrius professed to be as amazed as she had been at how generous the ordinary people of Magic City were and pitched in readily with carrying and loading the stuff the city was donating to the Abbey.

He hauled his part of the load up the steep hill without complaint, clearly entranced by both the picturesque walk and the sight of the abbey at the end of it. He said, "You know, I've lived here for a long time but never been up here. Of course, I know about it. Everyone does. Seeing it is somehow different."

Ruby nodded, thinking about how much she liked Demetrius's thoughtfulness and complete lack of fear about sharing his ideas. "I always have the same reaction. It seems almost unreal, like it radiates a sense of peace that gets inside you as you approach."

He grinned. "That's exactly it."

"When you meet Abbott Thomas, you'll understand. I don't think he's a magical, as such, but I do believe the way he shares his serenity is a kind of magic."

Demetrius laughed. "Plus, the beer."

Ruby nodded. "Of course. I do have a deep appreciation for that, as well."

They deposited their burdens, and Ruby took Demetrius on a tour of the Abbey, ending in the Brew Hall. Abbott Thomas was there, his long white hair pulled back in a ponytail, and his beard and mustache more closely trimmed than the last time she'd seen him. He exchanged handshakes with her boyfriend, and they talked for a few minutes about what infomancy was and how it worked.

Ruby watched their exchange and was struck as she always was at how the abbey's leader seemed to be genuinely interested, appeared to listen with every fiber of his being as if nothing in the universe could distract him. *That's what makes him seem so trustworthy, that laser focus. We're lucky to have him.* The abbot and those he led had helped her personally on many occasions, and she knew that what he did for the needy in the city was orders of magnitude greater. *So many people will never know how much he helped them. Which is probably exactly how he wants it.*

At a break in their conversation, Ruby interrupted, "Could we have a word with you in private?" She tilted her head toward the small room off the hall where they'd talked before. He nodded amicably and led them over. Once he shut the door, he asked, "What can I do for you?"

She replied, "Nothing at the moment, but you might want to have some extra hands around in general, and specifically some with medical experience."

His expression took on a darker cast. "May I ask why?"

"Indications are that something bad is going to happen in Magic City. Obviously, the authorities will do what they can to stop it. I'm trying to make sure we've got all our potential resources ready to go."

Thomas nodded. "That won't be too difficult. Do you have a timeframe?"

She shook her head. "People are working on it, but I have my doubts that we'll get one. This is probably a situation where we need to be ready as soon as possible and remain vigilant until we know the threat has passed."

He sighed and shook his head. "It's unfortunate folks can't just get along. I know, I know, it's a ridiculous expectation. Too many different perspectives, too many strong emotions. That doesn't stop me from wishing and praying for it."

Demetrius suggested, "Maybe you should start putting a sedative in your beer. Or something that makes people more tranquil and happy."

A smile overtook his face. "What's to say that I don't?" He laughed. "Not everyone drinks our brews, unfortunately."

Ruby said, "Hey, on that topic. A friend of mine came up with a great opportunity for you to get more taste buds on your creations and for my family's casino to benefit from it, too. I think you're going to like this idea."

CHAPTER TWENTY-FOUR

Ruby returned home that day to find that Keshalla had left her a note rather than a ribbon. It apologized for being unable to locate anyone to modify the artifact sword and suggested she contact people knowledgeable about magic items. She had immediately gone to visit Shentia and asked her for advice. A day later, she found herself in kemana Stonesreach, under the city of Pittsburgh, for the second time.

Nylotte had met her and Idryll at Shentia's and portaled them to a small storefront with a sword hanging over the door. The Drow led her inside, and Ruby was immediately surprised by how expensive the space looked inside. She remarked on it, and Nylotte laughed. "Alessand owns most of this block. He makes it look like a bunch of separate shops from the outside. At first, it was probably a desire not to be ostentatious. At this point, though, I think it's basically a game for him."

The room was full of weapons racks, covering all the walls other than the front windows and the two doors. They shone in the light of a chandelier that hung over the rectangular wooden island in the center of the room. The counter looked like someone had crafted it from a single block of wood. Ruby could happily spend hours examining the weapons on the walls and imagined Keshalla would drool at the sight of this place.

The man in question, presumably, stepped into view from a door on the back wall. The Dark Elf wore his long hair pulled back from his face. He seemed stronger looking than most Drow she'd seen, bulkier but still as elegant as any of his kind. His deep green tunic was embroidered with black designs and fell past his knees. It was slit on the sides to reveal black trousers underneath. He was, in a word, gorgeous.

He crossed the room and wrapped Nylotte in a hug, which she returned seemingly enthusiastically. Ruby blinked in surprise. Idryll whispered, "Well. That's unexpected."

"Right?" When they disengaged, she walked forward with her hand extended. "Hi. I'm Ruby Achera."

He shook it. "Alessand. Nylotte explained what you need, and I can most likely handle it. May I see the weapon?" She drew it partway from its sheath and offered him the hilt.

He took it from her and set it on the huge wooden block in the center of the space, then walked around it, his hands hovering an inch away from the sword, seeming almost to commune with it. "What is its name?"

"Eidolon."

He smiled. "Appropriate for a sentient weapon. Do you

have the inhabitant's permission to alter it in the way you've requested?"

The question surprised her. It wasn't something she'd considered or even thought of. The fact that he asked said a lot about his character if one presumed he would refuse to work on it if they disagreed. She nodded. "They suggested, well, agreed with the suggestion."

"They?"

Ruby replied, "Yes. There are two sentient beings in there. Separate. Generally on the same page."

He turned to look at Nylotte, who shrugged. "I've found her to be truthful."

He smiled at Ruby. "Okay, then. If Nylotte believes in you, I do too. Let's head to the back."

Idryll whispered, "I believe in you, too. I believe you're a chucklehead."

"Shut it, sherpa." She'd taken to using titles that Idryll specifically rejected in order to annoy her.

He escorted them into a workshop filled with various tools and workstations that were entirely foreign to her. He took the sword to one of them and clamped it into a holder at about chest height, with the blade pointing upward. He instructed, "Grip it like you're going to swing it, please." Ruby complied, and he guided her through holding it at multiple angles and in several ways, manipulating the holder to make each possible, and made dots on it each time with a Sharpie marker.

When they finished, several markings clustered around a certain space. Alessand said, "I had hoped to put the item where your pinky rests, but your fingers are kind of small, so that's not a good idea. Instead, we'll use your index finger, as your middle one seems to be an essential part of your grip."

She replied, "Okay. Whatever you say."

He nodded as if that was the right answer and crossed to something that resembled an apothecary cabinet with much smaller drawers. He returned with a small object and held it up so she could see it. "Think this'll do?"

Idryll asked, "Is that a diamond?"

Alessand nodded. "Yes. Seemed an appropriate choice for the *Mirra* of the Mist Elves. It's small enough that it won't penetrate far, but the point is sharp enough that it shouldn't be difficult to make the connection."

Nylotte frowned. "Is it durable?"

Alessand laughed. "It's a diamond, darling. The hardest substance on this planet. It is certainly *durable*."

The Drow woman scowled. "You know what I mean. Will it stay mounted where it belongs?"

He replied, "It should. I'll be bonding it directly with the sword's metal rather than adding it on with a mount. As long as those inside are truly in agreement with the process, it shouldn't affect the item's magic at all."

Ruby said, "Give me a moment to check one more time." She grabbed the hilt and fell into the mental space where she conversed with Shalia and Tyrsh. A second later, she opened her eyes. "They agree again."

He nodded with a smile. "Then let's make some magic."

It had been wonderful to watch the master at work, and when he finished, they tested it. Sure enough, by pushing her finger against the knob, she was able to send her magic spiraling through the sword. He said that eventually, she might not require the diamond anymore. In which case she should let him know, and he would remove the sharp edge from it but allow her to keep it as a decoration. She hadn't known how to thank him, and when she tried, he waved it away. "Helping you makes Nylotte happy. That's all the thanks I need for this small task."

Now that she was back in the bunker, she collapsed on the couch, setting the sheathed sword against its side. She leaned her head on the cushions and closed her eyes. "I think I need a vacation."

Idryll flopped down beside her. "That sounds like a great idea. Somewhere with a lake. A lake with fish."

Morrigan, who had already been in their secret base when they arrived, laughed. "Salmon aren't smoked in the water. You understand that, right?"

Idryll's voice was filled with scorn as if Ruby's sister was the dumbest person who ever spoke. "First, I'm sure they'd be delicious, regardless. Second, doubtless, there are other kinds of fish in a lake that might also be delicious. Third, as long as a store nearby has smoked salmon, I'll be fine."

Margrave's laugh preceded him into the room, and Ruby opened her eyes as he threw a butcher-paper-wrapped package at the shapeshifter. "Your wish for delish fish is hereby granted."

Idryll caught it and tore into the wrapping immediately. Ruby asked, "Where's mine?"

The technomancer hefted the bag he carried over his shoulder. "I thought you might like a different kind of gift."

Morrigan frowned. "What about me?"

He laughed. "There's something in here for you, too, never fear." Ruby and Morrigan escorted him into the work area while Idryll sat on the couch and devoured the smoked salmon he'd provided. Margrave remarked, "She's mostly cat, isn't she."

Ruby nodded. "Near as I can tell."

Morrigan added, "And the part that isn't is pure sass."

Ruby countered, "Which is also more or less catlike behavior. It must be the attitude that makes the two of you get along so well.

Her sister stuck out her tongue. "If you were smarter, you could be sassier, too."

Margrave chuckled. "Okay, friends. I have some paying work to get back to, so let's get this done." He reached into the bag and set four arrowheads on the table.

Ruby complained, "Why does she get to go first?"

"Because these were at the top of the bag. Hush." He pointed at the two that had red circles engraved near the tip. "These are dangerous. Seriously dangerous. You're going to want to be careful with them."

Morrigan replied, "Oh. All right." Her voice had turned less playful. "Tell me more."

"They go active two seconds after the accelerometer detects their launch. They discharge bursts of microwaves that act as heat when it touches electronics."

Her sister frowned. "Okay, so?"

Margrave sighed. "This is one of those things the Army would really like that I'm never going to give them. You should only use them in a life-or-death situation." Ruby's curiosity was piqued, and while she thought she should be able to figure out why they were so deadly, it wasn't coming to her.

Morrigan nodded, looking concerned. "I get it. Because?"

"They will activate any detonators or explosives that are heat sensitive. So, not devices that use a plunger, but just about any others. Microwaves can also trigger ones waiting for a current."

Her sister breathed, "Holy hell."

Ruby echoed her and said, "I can see where you don't want this getting out."

He nodded. "These are the only two in existence. My notes and formulas are in the secure repository your boyfriend set up for me. The hardware in the arrow will self-destruct after six seconds, basically burning out all the electronics so no one can reverse-engineer them. Still, if you can retrieve them, that would be good."

Her sister looked a little sick at the new addition to her arsenal. "Yeah. I'll do that." She pointed at the ones with the blue tip. "What do they do?"

"Ultra-localized EMP. Literally only good for about a foot. So, whatever equipment you want to kill, you'll have to hit it."

Morrigan said the obligatory, "My precious," but Ruby could see she was still intimidated by the detonator activators.

Margrave reached into the bag again and dropped a collection of discs onto Ruby's workbench, smaller than the ones they currently used but otherwise identical. He said, "Explosive, knockout gas, and smoke."

Ruby shrugged. "Cool. But not nearly as impressive as

what you gave her. You've always liked my sister more, haven't you?"

He nodded with a serious expression, but his flat tone indicated he was joking. "Yes. I always have. I just used you to get to her." He shook his head and withdrew what looked like a metal cylinder from the bag and handed it to her. She gripped it in her left hand, testing its weight. "So. It's a pipe. For bashing with, I suppose? Bashing magicals with a magical basher?"

He sighed and said, "It's heavy and strong so you can use it to block. More importantly, it's a way to channel your magic. You can cast shadow through it without a problem. Don't use fire. It'll melt the components. Force might be problematic, too, so I'd avoid it unless truly necessary. What you really want it for is lightning."

Ruby hefted it again and peered at it curiously. "Why?"

"Because it has a series of capacitors inside. Charge it before you go into battle, and it will increase the power of what you send out while limiting its spread based on the shape. Basically, your lightning will hit fewer people but be much more powerful when cast through there."

Ruby twirled it. "Can I test it on Morrigan?"

He shook his head. "I wouldn't recommend it. You should trust me on this one."

"Thanks, Margrave. Seriously."

He nodded. "Be careful. You are my favorite protégé, and I'd like the opportunity to work with you on ludicrously profitable technomancer projects sometime."

She laughed. "Hopefully soon." *Yeah, hopefully. First, we have to figure out what the widow Sloane is up to and make sure she doesn't succeed.*

CHAPTER TWENTY-FIVE

Julianna Sloane descended the stairs from the private jet she'd chartered and climbed into the back of a stretch limousine that awaited her on the tarmac. The autonomous vehicle pulled away immediately after she entered, as they'd said it would. It had taken no less than ten calls, climbing the ladder through various lieutenants and security interventions, before she was able to get a meeting with the man and woman she was on the way to see. Even then, they'd insisted that they would host her rather than accepting her invitation to visit. *When my husband was alive, they would've come to him and been happy to do so. Things have definitely changed.*

She leaned back and closed her eyes, resigned to whatever events fate delivered to her in the next few hours. For all she knew, the whole thing could be a trap, and the limo would blow up on the way there. But she didn't think so. Eliminating her provided no benefit to them and working with her offered the potential for profit. *More profit than I'd like, I'm guessing. That, too, is a worry for later.*

When the car rolled to a stop and the door opened automatically, she stepped into an underground parking garage. She presumed she was still somewhere in Los Angeles, but for all she knew they'd driven through a portal, and she was halfway across the world. It didn't matter where she was, as long as she got to talk to who she needed to talk to.

A pair of bulky men in dark suits awaited her. The first said, "Welcome, Mrs. Sloane." The other said, "Mr. and Mrs. Carillo are expecting you." They escorted her to an elevator and inserted a key card into an unobtrusive slot at the side of the interior panel. The car smoothly accelerated upward.

It opened into a living room. She stepped out and smiled involuntarily. It reminded her of their place in Reno, the floor-to-ceiling windows offering a spectacular view of the city skyline. A voice from her right said, "Julianna, thank you for coming."

She turned and smiled at Stacia. The woman was elegant, tall and thin, almost a little too thin, to judge by the sunken cheeks. Her red hair cascaded down over her shoulders, and her lipstick matched it almost perfectly. A black dress hugged her in the appropriate places. "The pleasure's all mine. Thank you for agreeing to meet with me."

A man's voice from behind her replied, "We couldn't refuse a call from The Nightmare's wife. It wouldn't be polite."

She spun slowly and nodded at Carlo. Where his wife was beautiful, he was ruggedly handsome but would never be called pretty. His strong face featured rough skin, and bushy eyebrows and mustache gave the impression he didn't care too much about his looks most of the time. The expensive suit he wore would argue that he did, making him a bit of a paradox. "Nor would it be appropriate, given all my husband did for you while he was alive."

The other woman said, "So true. Care to have a seat and a drink?"

Julianna smiled. "I would be foolish to decline either." The living room was similar in layout to the one she and Gabriel had shared, though her hosts had chosen an abundance of comfortable chairs instead of the couches she'd preferred. They formed a horseshoe around an oval coffee table.

Two bottles of champagne were chilling in a silver bucket, and Carlo popped the cork on one and poured a glass for each of them. As he took his seat, he asked, "What can we do for you?"

Julianna sipped the sparkling wine, which was excellent. *Naturally.* "I'm looking to cause some serious destruction. A couple of casinos."

Stacia replied calmly, "Not in Vegas."

She shook her head. "Ely. Magic City."

Carlo said, "Of course. Do they still need to be standing afterward? Explosives are easily used and easily sourced."

Julianna sipped again. "One should be preserved, if at all possible. I don't care what happens to the other. If it survives, great. If it doesn't, fine. In either case, the action must happen in a way that strikes fear into the casino owners."

Stacia said, "Because you want them to sell or leave?"

She nodded. "Exactly. Or, should they die during the event, so much the better."

Carlo leaned back in his chair. "Doable. But it will cost you."

Julianna stifled the sigh that threatened to escape. "Of course. I understand. However, given the long-term relationship you had with my husband and the role he played in at the start of your career, I hope you'll be reasonable."

The other woman laughed. "When have we ever been reasonable?"

Carlo grinned. "You're correct. We owe a lot to The Nightmare, and we haven't forgotten that obligation. So, we'll accept forty-nine percent of your business in Magic City, whatever that turns out to be. In addition, sixty percent of your existing revenues until you've reimbursed our expenses for this operation."

A chill washed through her, which she concealed by taking another drink of her wine. She'd known it would be costly and had assumed it would be more than she wanted to give up. But those numbers were excessive even when compared to what she'd imagined the worst-case scenario to be. *Gabriel was right. Negotiating from the weaker position is a terrible thing.* She shook her head. "Impossible. I have obligations other than this operation and that significant a concession would render me unable to live up to them. As you know, promises made must be kept."

He nodded neutrally. "Indeed. What, then, would you consider more equitable?"

Julianna replied, "Let's say forty-five percent of the business in Magic City. That will be essentially found money, so I'm certainly willing to share it. However, my controlling interest must be more than a single percent."

Carlo refilled her glass and did the same for Julianna's. "I would say that's doable, depending on the rest of the package."

Julianna nodded. She'd figured that wouldn't be the sticking point. "And the same number on the existing revenues. However, I know that won't meet your needs. So, I suggest that once we handle our business in Magic City, we create a formal alliance between your organization and mine. Mutual benefit, mutual defense, shared decision-making in Ely. I would get a voice here, but obviously as a minority partner. That increases the risk, I understand, but also dramatically raises the potential reward."

He tapped his fingers on the edge of the glass as he considered the offer. "Possible. But we would require assurances. You are aware of what that would entail, are you not?"

Julianna nodded. *Yes, unfortunately.* "I am. Please make sure my future husband is attractive and intelligent. The latter is more important than the former."

Stacia laughed. "Oh, I don't know. Pretty and dumb can be quite appealing."

Carlo smiled. "Fortunately, I have a brother of each variety. You can get to know them and choose which you prefer."

Julianna nodded. "I think we have an agreement."

He replied, "Agreed."

Stacia confirmed, "Agreed."

Carlo rose from his chair and extended a hand. "I'm looking forward to working with you, Julianna. Give my people the details, and we'll get back to you within a day on plans and possibilities." The security guards arrived to escort her to the limo, and it moved as soon as the door closed.

She was confident there would be no double-cross now and that her next stop would be at the airport for her return to Magic City. *A promised betrothal is definitely more than I wanted to give. But then, Magic City is a dangerous place, and I have oh-so-many enemies. I've become a widow once. I'm sure that enduring it a second time won't be nearly as painful.*

She closed her eyes and leaned back in the comfortable seat, imagining methods of dispatching an unwanted spouse, her satisfied smile growing larger as the scenarios grew more elaborate. *Oh yes. I think Magic City could very well turn out to be an exceedingly dangerous home for my next husband.*

CHAPTER TWENTY-SIX

Ruby, Idryll, and Morrigan crouched under a veil on the rooftop of Invention casino. Three of Demetrius's drones were up there with them, guaranteeing a view in all directions around the structure. Morrigan said, "I still think you're wrong. It will be at The Underground."

Ruby sighed. Her sister had been sharing that particular conclusion repeatedly since the moment they'd all connected on comms. If it were only the three of them, that would be one thing. All sorts of people were on tonight's party line, though. They'd included Grentham and his most trusted lieutenants. That had been a challenge to arrange, but she'd had Demetrius ask Scimitar to handle it, arguably keeping her identity secret. *At this point, what will be will be with him.*

Prex and several of the Desert Ghosts were on as well, riding the streets near the Strip. One other member of the biker club was present, acting as the information collector for the ones inside the casinos. Demetrius, Kayleigh, and even Scimitar rounded out the group, although after confirming her presence, the enigmatic infomancer hadn't spoken.

Ruby said, "For the hundredth time, you might be right, but we're going to stay here. You can portal us over there in like, a second. So, chill."

Morrigan replied, "I'm just saying. Maybe that's where our eyes should be looking."

Demetrius intoned dramatically, "My eyes are everywhere."

Ruby laughed. "Thanks, D. Regardless of her babbling, Barb knows you have it under control."

Her sister confirmed, "That's true. I'm not questioning your judgment. Only hers."

He countered, "And the fact that we agree with her doesn't matter?"

Morrigan confirmed, "Not a bit."

Chuckles sounded from over the comms. Then it was time for another round of confirmations. Ruby said, "DG-one?"

Prex replied, "Nothing from me and mine on the outside." He would be the funnel for all the information from the motorcycle patrol unless something went seriously wrong and instant notice was required from one of his people.

"DG-two?"

Prex's second in command, Violet, was coordinating the reports from the people inside the casinos. "Nothing suspicious."

"Grentham."

"In position, ready to roll on either one." The dwarf had put together all of his security people who weren't currently working security and spread them out on the Strip. He'd also included some other folks, probably from the pawnshops he owned. Ruby wasn't entirely comfortable with his participation but had been worried enough about what Julianna Sloane might be up to that she'd set that concern aside.

"D."

Her boyfriend replied, "Fully operational, nothing to see yet."

"Glam?"

Diana Sheen's tech was piloting at least one of the Agents' heavy drones in the area. She'd explained that the craft was stealthy enough that they wouldn't have to worry about anyone noticing it was in use. Ruby wasn't all that comfortable with the situation, but turning away assistance seemed like a bad plan. Kayleigh replied, "Nominal."

Finally, she said, "Scimitar?"

A small momentary burst of static was the only response. At first, she'd thought something was wrong, but after several iterations, Grentham had explained that sometimes the infomancer used that as an acknowledgment. Ruby had connected only to him and asked, "Why?"

He'd only sighed. "No idea. She's unique. You sort of take what you get."

With the cycle complete, Idryll said, "This waiting is endlessly boring. I wish something would get started."

Ruby replied, "We don't even know that it will happen tonight." They'd brought the full team into the field at Scimitar's urging. The infomancer hadn't shared specifics, only indicated that circumstances were right for a move. The previous few nights had included some of the assembled players, but not all of them, watching, waiting, and fretting.

She was mentally counting off the seconds until it would be time to do another round of check-ins when Prex's excited voice said, "Several identical box trucks spotted. They're present on both sides of the Strip."

Demetrius announced, "Redeploying," and the three drones sharing the roof with them buzzed away.

Ruby said, "Cat, take the left corner. Barb, the right." Her partners split off to regain two of the perspectives they'd lost, and Ruby waited anxiously for more information.

Prex reported, "They look like rentals or used fleet buys. Bright yellow."

The infomancer's synthesized voice answered instantly, "Checking. License plates will help. Taking over the traffic cameras now."

They'd not wanted to risk the Ely PD finding out what they were up to any earlier than necessary. Everyone was in agreement that the local police department had issues where security was concerned, either deliberately because they were on the take or simply because they were unlucky enough not to be as well-funded as those who would seek to exploit them. *Speaking of exploitation.* Ruby said, "D, bring Andrews and his people in."

"You sure?"

"Yeah. If those trucks have explosives, things could get bad really quick."

In her other ear, the one reserved for direct communications rather than the party line, Morrigan offered, "If there are explosives, I can take them out whenever. But the collateral damage, I don't know."

Ruby didn't share her sister's certainty about her new arrows. She knew they were a bad idea. "You keep those things sheathed. Quivered. Whatever. They're a total last resort option."

Kayleigh broke in and said, "I've got my drone on the one nearest *Spirits* casino, which was closest to its position." That wasn't an accident. The tech had decided to keep it close to her family's place, and Ruby was very thankful for it. Kayleigh sounded slightly confused when she reported, "It's empty."

Prex muttered, "Clever. It's a shell game. Some are diversions. Some are real."

Idryll chuckled. "Classic."

Ruby asked, "How can we differentiate?"

Kayleigh said, "Rambo is with me, and he said something about the Italian Job."

Scimitar replied, "Right. Laden trucks will ride lower because they're heavier. Checking."

The tech replied, "Me too."

Demetrius said, "Me three."

Ruby's hands flexed open and closed, the nervous energy needing an escape before it boiled out of her. The mention of explosives had shot adrenaline through her system. Plus, the fact that after multiple nights of no results things were finally happening had her keyed up beyond the ability to stay still. *I should have asked Daphne to make some kind of relaxation capsules, too.*

Kayleigh said, "Found one. Scanning now. Thermal

blooms consistent with bodies. Scanner suggests there's a dozen of them in there, not including the driver."

Ruby asked, "Where are they headed?"

Demetrius replied, "No pattern detected."

The status quo held for almost a minute before Prex reported, "Three of them just changed direction abruptly." Kayleigh, Demetrius, and Scimitar all confirmed that about half of the vehicles they were tracking had done the same —the ones filled with people.

Scimitar said, "Two appear to be heading for Invention. Eight inbound to The Underground."

Ruby felt the blood rush toward her feet, chilling her all the way down. "Where the hell did they get that many people?" She shook her head. "Ignore that question. Doesn't matter. Scimitar, evacuate both casinos. Grentham, you and your people head to Invention. D, send the PDA there, too. We're heading for The Underground."

CHAPTER TWENTY-SEVEN

Morrigan's portal took them to an alley that ran alongside The Underground. One of Grentham's security personnel opened the door at their arrival, and they bustled in, running through the backstage areas of the casino. Ruby demanded, "Status?"

Demetrius replied, "I'm in the casino's cameras. Enemies flooding in through both front entrances. Lots of them. Black masks, black outfits, body armor. Rifles."

Grentham snapped, "Worldspan?"

She rolled her eyes as she ran. *He's got a serious preoccupation with those folks.* Demetrius answered, "Unknown."

Scimitar added, "Multiple encrypted communication bands running. Could be more than one group acting independently. Comm signals at Invention don't match either of the others."

Kayleigh summarized, "So, three teams, probably operating autonomously but with at least one person in each who connects back to a central control at need. That's how we'd run it."

Prex asked, "Do you need us inside?"

Ruby replied, "No chance. You've done the most important part. Pull all your people out and maintain a loose perimeter. If anyone tries to run, we'll turn to you for help." He responded in the affirmative, and she continued, "D, when you have the bandwidth, tag the vehicles." That would let them trace the trucks with Margrave's equipment.

"On it."

They burst through the doors onto the casino floor. Ruby had been waiting for a camera feed into her lenses, but once she saw what was going on, she was happy Demetrius hadn't supplied one in advance. She couldn't have run faster, and it would have only made her more anxious. The invaders were shooting everything that moved. Patrons, workers, guards, whoever; people were going down left and right. As she grew closer, she identified some intention in the melee and scowled. "They're focusing mainly on killing dwarves. The folks making it to the exits all seem to be humans, elves, whatever."

Morrigan growled, "Damned scumbags."

Grentham snarled, "More evidence it's the widow behind this. She has a reason to dislike my people."

She has a reason to dislike you, you mean, and is evil enough to take it out on all the dwarves. Ruby ordered, "Cat, Barb, let's beat these bastards down. Focus on supporting the guards and eliminating the greatest threats first."

Morrigan asked, "*Eliminating* eliminating?"

Ruby weighed the odds, confirming that they were downright horrible. "Do your best to remain nonlethal.

Same rules as always though. If you need to go harder to stay alive, do it."

Kayleigh said, "My drone's on patrol, circling the building. If they get up to anything outside, I'll take them down."

Scimitar reported, "The buildings are mostly evacuated. Fire and rescue have deployed. Sheriff and PD on the way."

Demetrius added, "Also, a huge wave of PDA drones is inbound. Watch out for them."

Ruby nodded. The Agency wasn't afraid to bring their hardware inside, and things would be moving fast enough that they'd be a threat to enemy and ally alike. With all the boxes she could think of checked, she was free to take some direct action. She drew her sword and the pipe Margrave had given her and shouted, "Let's get them."

Morrigan fired her grapnel at the railing of the second-floor balcony and flew upward under a veil. She climbed over it and drew her bow, her other hand searching for the appropriate arrow for the moment as the weapon unfolded. When the bowstring zipped into place, she had her projectile ready, and it took only a second to fit it, draw, and fire.

The flashbang arrow arced to land in one of the casino entrances, at least momentarily lessening the flow of enemies. Another of the same type flew into a cluster of black-suited troops who had formed a small triangle with their backs to one another and were firing seemingly at random in all directions.

She followed that one up with a knockout gas arrow to

the same target, unconcerned with the fact that her attack might catch innocents as well. The likelihood that she would save someone by knocking them out was far greater than her action putting them in additional danger, especially if it also took out the people most likely to hurt them.

Morrigan distributed her two remaining knockout gas arrows into clusters of attackers, then grabbed a lightning one. A bullet smacked into her vest, knocking her back a step as she released the string, messing up her shot. The lightning arrow struck a few feet away from where she'd intended, but the electricity it discharged still snagged several enemies and sent them twitching to the floor, at least dazed, possibly unconscious. *Out of the fight for a bit, anyway.*

More bullets slammed into the ceiling over her head as she summoned a veil. She ran to a new location, then peered over the side, looking for whoever had shot at her. A set of five enemies were clustered in the middle, seemingly working together. Four surrounded the fifth, who was the one with the pistol raised at the second level. Their black uniforms were a little different than the ones around the casino floor, and their vests looked longer and better designed. "We've got an elite unit of some kind in here."

Grentham asked immediately, "Worldspan?"

Ruby snarled, "Not every enemy is Worldspan." She brought her voice back to normal. "How are things at Invention?"

He replied, "Fine, almost under control. Only about half of them made it in before we arrived. My people are holding them at bay."

Idryll said, "Wish we could say the same about your folks here."

"I'm on my way."

Morrigan scowled. *That's a bad idea, but he's not going to listen.* She released her veil and selected another of the lightning arrows. She fired it at the shooter, and it deflected from an invisible barrier a couple of feet away from her target. "Dammit, they've got a magical."

Idryll said, "I see them. Don't worry. My claws don't care about their magic."

<hr>

Idryll charged the fivesome laying waste to everything around them in the center of the casino floor. A slot machine sparked and smoked nearby, and the closest blackjack table was splintered and broken. She cataloged her foes automatically as she dashed in, her partially shifted form carrying her faster than any human would be able to run. *Two with shotguns, two with rifles, one with only a pistol. But she's the magical, for sure.*

She was aware that more than one of them could be magical, but it didn't matter in the least to her approach. Idryll was deep into her combat zone, and she would deal with each challenge as it appeared, letting reflexes and instinct guide her. She leapt at the woman from a distance she thought her escorts wouldn't anticipate, but the guards around her target smoothly repositioned themselves to intervene.

A shotgun raised in her direction, but she was coming too fast for the wielder to get the angle he needed, and his shot missed. Her claws sliced the barrel in two, and she smashed into the shooter, knocking him back toward the one in the center.

The woman shuffled forward to avoid getting bumped and cast a fireball up at the balcony. Idryll saw Morrigan ignore the incoming projectile, calmly drawing another arrow and fitting it to her bowstring. The attack dissipated as the archer's magic deflector drank in the power. She quipped, "Aww. Did your fancy spell not work?" The figure didn't reply, only swung her pistol around and pulled the trigger.

Idryll dropped and took a smash on the jaw from the butt of another one's rifle on the way down. It sent tiny embers floating through her vision. She shook her head to clear it and came up from her crouch in a double punch at the one who'd hit her. Her fists connected with the person's chest and broke their bones, the enhanced strength from her partial transformation mostly negating any protection the bulletproof vest might have offered. Idryll refocused on the magical, but her target dashed off, headed for the far side of the casino.

She yelled, "Don't run," but then immediately had to dive and roll as another shotgun fired in her direction. The weapon continued to blaze at her, forcing her to keep running away from her quarry. She growled, "They chased me off. Someone else is going to have to handle that person."

Grentham's voice growled, "I saw the whole thing. It's Prash from Worldspan. I know how the wench moves by now. She's mine. Someone clear me a path."

CHAPTER TWENTY-EIGHT

Ruby muttered curses in annoyance but moved to do as the dwarf had requested. *Clear a path, sure. No problem, buddy. Not like I have anything else to do.* She strode forcefully toward her destination, engaging each enemy she found along the way. Her sword was in her right hand, and she gripped the pipe weapon Margrave had created in her left.

A man appeared in her path with an assault rifle aimed at her chest, and she pointed the pipe at him and sent magic into it. Lightning burst from the opening, wreathing him and dropping him to the floor instantly, without what she usually thought of as "twitch time." She presumed he was unconscious and not dead because Margrave would have made the weapon nonlethal, knowing the rules they were operating under in relation to the Sheriff's office.

She lacked time to check and be sure because *she had to clear a path.* She sighed at herself. *Quit being a drama queen, Ruby, and get your ass in gear.* She siphoned magic into the pipe to charge up the internal capacitors again and skipped forward to slash her sword down at the barrel of a shotgun. It knocked the weapon out of line and caused the enemy to shoot one of his teammates. That unlucky figure went down with a cry, and she slid ahead and smashed the hilt of Eidolon into the shooter's face. He staggered backward instead of falling, so she spun into a back kick that brought her heel into his temple. *Then* he fell, and she continued.

Tyrsh and Shalia murmured in her mind, warning her of enemies that she might not have seen. They weren't all on the same wavelength quite yet, as the duo often shared things she already knew. She'd mentioned that to Nylotte after Alessand had altered her sword, and the Drow had simply replied, "Practice." *Clearly cut from the same cloth as Keshalla.*

Her lightning took out two more enemies that tried to stop her at a distance. Then she was forced to defend herself from a barrage of shadow bolts sent by a masked figure that looked no different than the others. She swung her sword in a circle, summoning a force shield to protect the front of her body. The shadow bolts impacted and dispersed, and she fired lightning at the caster through a small gap in her shield.

It met a shield in return. Ruby dashed forward, sending another blast of electricity high to draw her opponent's defenses upward and ramming out her foot to catch the other magical in the stomach. She growled, "Fancy spells are only half the game, scumbag." The masked head tilted up toward her from the figure's doubled-over position, and she punched it with her right fist, angled, so the stun knuckles discharged and dropped her enemy.

The person Grentham claimed was Angelina Prash

from Worldspan launched a fireball at Ruby. She countered with blasts of ice from her sword and her pipe. Where the two elements met, they canceled each other out and sent a light shower of rain falling on everyone beneath.

A slot machine exploded to her left, and she side-stepped away from it, slightly off balance. It happened again and again as Prash and her escort took advantage of her surroundings to create a barrier between them. She growled, "I can't get closer safely. She sucks."

Grentham replied, "Not a problem. You did enough. Leave the wench to me."

Grentham hurled the ax in his right hand at one of the people ahead of him, and it buried itself in the back of Prash's remaining guard's head. The figure fell, and he yanked the weapon free without pausing as he strode by, flicking it to clear the blood from the blade and sheathing it on his left side. The surrounding battle had fallen into a hazy mist. He no longer cared about any part of it other than eliminating the woman before him.

A portion of his mind maintained a protective force shield around him with several layers to blunt any attack that penetrated the first. He'd brought along one helper to guard his back and was confident she'd be able to keep him safe from anyone who might want to interfere with his third round against the elven wench in charge of Worldspan. He called, "Take off that mask. We all know who you are."

She spun and laughed. "Grentham. I should've figured."

She complied, confirming it was Prash underneath. "Quite a mess your security company has made of things here, yet again."

"This will be the end of yours, too."

She shook her head. "I'm only here to help defend the place because Aces is so deeply, unforgivably incompetent. Trust me when I say that all the security footage they'll be able to pull afterward will confirm that."

He muttered, "Scimitar, hear that?"

The infomancer replied, "I've been downloading the feed all along. Don't worry."

He grinned. "Yeah, we'll see how that works out for your company. Or, more specifically, *I'll* see how that works out for your company. You'll be dead, so I guess you won't care either way."

Prash taunted, "Think you can make that happen, little man?"

He nodded once. "Yeah. Pretty sure of it."

Her reply was to send a force blast into the nearest slot machine, launching it at his skull. He sheathed his left-hand ax and cast force bolts of his own to knock it away with a shake of his head. "Pedestrian."

Prash growled, "Just getting warmed up, worm." A sound from above warned him. He shuffle-stepped to the side, almost dancing out of the way of the chandelier that crashed where he'd stood. He laughed. "Really? You're not all that impressive when you don't have the chance to prepare the battlefield ahead of time. Should I wait while you get some reinforcements to make it a fair fight?"

She lifted the gun and emptied the magazine at him, to no avail. He'd been keeping an eye out for defensive options, and the huge metal base of a roulette wheel protected his head from the bullets, while his vest and leg armor protected the rest of him from what were surely anti-magic rounds. He let the improvised shield fall as she holstered the weapon, not bothering to attempt to reload it. *Smart. I'd have detached her arm from her body if she'd tried.*

She moved to her left, toward the edge of the room, and he paralleled the motion. "You won't escape again, wench."

She shook her head. "Not trying to. I'd prefer a clear area where I can beat the life out of you at leisure."

"You offer lots of talk, but not much action. In the words of Mr. Blonde, are you going to bark all day, little doggy?"

She replied by snatching at her belt and throwing a canister at him. He smacked it aside with a wave of force magic, and it flew through the air before exploding and sending shrapnel everywhere. She shook her head. "Damn, you really don't care about anyone but yourself, do you?"

"I'm not the one tossing frag grenades." *I thought it was something magical. Dammit.* The context around their fight was starting to seep into his mental space. The fact that wounded and injured nearby needed attention was a problem, and while he dallied with Prash, the other invaders kept mowing people down. He said, "You know, I'd really enjoy making this last. But I think I'll wrap it up quickly instead, so I can stop all the damage your friends are doing to people who don't deserve it."

She gave a short laugh. "You can try. And they're not my friends."

"Whatever. You might want to reload that gun." He grabbed his belt and pulled out the anti-magic emitter he and Jared had figured out how to recharge. He threw it at her feet as he dashed in. She looked shocked as she lost her power, then grabbed her pistol and the spare magazine in her vest. He smashed her face with his ax, surprised to discover after the fact that he'd used the blunt side rather than the blade.

He drove his left fist into her shoulder, hoping to numb out her main arm, then whipped his right-hand ax around low, slamming it into her left shin. Bone *crunched* as it fractured or shattered, and she fell to the floor howling. He kicked her in the head to silence her, then stood with the ax in his hand, trembling with the desire to finish her off. Finally, he took a step backward. "You're not worth the stain on my soul. Besides, it'll be fun visiting you in jail and reminding you of everything you're missing on the outside."

He turned and strode away, looking for someone to save.

Ruby slammed the flat of her blade against her opponent's head, dropping the person who'd fired three bullets into her vest, which wasn't a problem, and one into her shoulder, which was. She slapped the healing potion and grimaced as it expelled the bullet. "Status."

Morrigan said, "Looks like we've got things under control in here. The security forces have rallied and are pushing the invaders back. They're still breaking everything they can, naturally, but what's important is there are no more innocents here to hurt. Only combatants on the battlefield, now."

Idryll reported, "A bunch of them are down. I haven't had to kill anyone. I saw Grentham take out one of the leaders, so that's under control, too."

Ruby frowned. "Well, okay then. That's unexpected." It seemed like things had gone from critical to controlled faster than expected, which made her suspicious.

Kayleigh's words came fast as if she was alarmed. "You need to get outside. I think the thing in there was only the prelude."

Ruby ran for the door as ice filled her veins.

CHAPTER TWENTY-NINE

Ruby dashed out of the casino and onto the Strip, sure that she'd find a bunch of black-clad enemies waiting for her. Her run slowed to a walk. Then she stopped moving entirely, her brain going completely offline as she stared up at the monstrous creature standing before her. Idryll stepped into place at her side and said, "Is that a crocodile?"

Ruby shook her head slowly. "The head is, anyway. The body looks more like a T-Rex, but with normal-sized arms."

Morrigan, breathing heavily as she arrived, asked, "By normal size, you mean, what, like two or three school buses?"

Ruby frowned, still unable to grasp the creature in front of her. "Well, it's proportional. That thing must be what, twenty stories tall?"

The beast was mammoth, like something out of a science-fiction movie. It was indeed almost half the height of The Underground's hotel tower. It was easy to make the comparison because it was actively engaged with the structure, raining punches down on it like it had insulted its mother. Ruby's brain involuntarily tried to put together the picture of a crocodile and a dinosaur mating, and she shut that process down *fast. Some things absolutely do* not *bear thinking about.*

The monster's body thrashed from side to side as it boxed the tower, which caused its huge tail to sweep aside vehicles and defenders on the Strip. Armored scales covered its skin, greenish-black or blackish green. She couldn't tell which. *Muddy river colors.*

Her brain finally cleared as the inhabitants of her sword caught her attention. She sensed they'd been yelling at her for a while. "Yeah, right. Sorry. I didn't expect to see," she gestured with the tip of the sword, "that." She shook her head, clearing the last cobwebs. "Okay, so it's big, and it's bad, and it's downright freaking scary, but it still needs to go down. Drones?"

Demetrius replied, "I've got nothing with armaments aboard. The PDA has been strafing it but to no apparent effect. The call has gone out to the military, but it's going to be a little while before they can get here."

"Grentham, how about sending some of your people to the closest base to portal them straight to the Strip? Might save some time."

He replied, "On it. I'm not sure what my folks can do against this thing."

Ruby shook her head. "Me neither. Get clear. This one's not your fight. Work on getting reinforcements here as quickly as possible."

"You got it."

Kayleigh said, "Let's see if this does any damage."

Demetrius put the feed from the tech's drone in her left lens, and Ruby watched as it dove in on the creature with larger-than-normal bullets streaming out ahead of it. They deflected from the scales around its eye, and the thing jerked its head away before the drone could strike that potentially vulnerable spot.

Its tail whipped up from off-screen, was momentarily visible in the camera, then the feed was gone. Ruby saw the explosion in her other lens as it destroyed the craft. "That Crocosaur is nasty."

Demetrius replied, "Crocosaur. Really?"

"Not now, D. Okay, Idryll, with me. We'll go after its feet and see if claws and sword can do any good. Morrigan, you're a free agent. I'd suggest going up high, try to put an arrow in its eye or its mouth or something. Prex, get your people the hell out of here."

She strode forward and had a thought. "Scimitar, have we confirmed that we accounted for all the vehicles? There's not one with explosives waiting to blow up a casino?"

The infomancer replied, "All those we detected are indeed accounted for."

"Good." Ruby crossed that off her list of concerns. "Well, we're down to one problem. That's something, right?"

Morrigan laughed. "I guess that's one way to look at it. It's a *big* problem, though. Be careful. Don't let it step on you."

She stared at the behemoth and shook her head in continued disbelief. "Yeah. Good point. I'll do my best."

Idryll transformed fully into her tiger form, that being the most powerful of her attack options. Her mask slipped down to hang around her neck, and the belt retracted so as not to be a hindrance. If the explosives discs proved to work, she could change back afterward to use hers. She was confident Ruby would test them, eventually.

At the moment, she had only one tried-and-true tactic in mind, to get behind the thing's feet and slice them into ribbons. Presumably, since it was upright, it had something resembling an Achilles tendon. If it did, it would likely be as vulnerable to damage as a human in that particular spot. *Well, minus the armor and the potential for getting squashed if I don't keep moving.*

She accelerated, trusting Ruby to take care of herself. She wondered on occasion if the relationship between previous companions and *Mirra* had been the same as theirs. Her frequent instinct was to protect her partner, but mostly Ruby wasn't interested in being protected. She wanted someone to complement her skills, which was an ideal role for Idryll. *I'm more an attacker than a defender when you come right down to it. I'm a tiger, after all.*

She wove between the wreckage of drones as they fell from the sky. The PDA was fully in the fight, at least with their machines, to judge by some of the disabled craft in her path. *Good, about time they did something useful.*

As she got close, the thing lifted its foot, and she skidded to a stop, waiting for some indication of what direction it would take. The huge leg moved toward the casino, so she dashed the other way, circling it. It came down on top of a police car whose occupant had wisely abandoned the vehicle and caused it to explode.

When the creature didn't lift his foot as a fireball erupted beneath it, Idryll's concern jumped up an order of magnitude. She dashed around to the rear of the foot and launched herself in the air, using all the power she had. She put every bit of muscle she possessed into a claw swipe across the back of its foot at the pinnacle of her leap.

Her natural weapons had never failed to penetrate anything when she'd delivered such a strike—stone, wood, metal. None of them had been fully able to resist her power. As her razor-sharp claws scraped off the scales, shock from the impact radiated up the limb and simultaneously erupted in her mind. She landed in a skid and turned, staring at the space she'd attacked. She hadn't damaged the scales at all. *Not even a damn scratch.* She bolted away and switched back into partial humanoid form. "My best shot did nothing to it. We're in trouble."

Morrigan had portaled to the roof of the next casino tower over and used her grapnel to drop down the side of the building to a height a couple of stories above the thing's head. She pushed off the wall and let herself swing toward a window, smashing the glass with a burst of force a second before she passed through.

She landed in a slide and hit the button to release the grapnel, turning back to the broken window as the cable automatically re-spooled into her belt. Morrigan snarled at the half-dressed couple scrambling out of bed. "Get the hell out of here. Aren't you paying attention to *anything* other than yourselves? Like all that banging and crashing? Idiots."

She drew her bow and grabbed an explosive arrow, firing it at the Crocosaur's head. The thing was in motion, so she missed the eye; her arrow detonated on the side of its face. It didn't seem to care. "Well, that's discouraging. My explosive arrow didn't do anything, either."

Ruby reminded her, "The eyes."

Morrigan scowled even though her sister couldn't see it. "Tell you what, you climb it and stick your sword in its eye, Miss Know It All. It's kind of hard to hit that target from this distance."

Her sister replied, "Excuses," and Morrigan lowered the bow, realizing she'd drawn her last explosive arrow. *Need to wait for my opening and make this one count.*

She put it back and tried the other arrow types in her quiver, aiming each time for the eye. None of them struck true as the creature thrashed about, and none did any damage. PDA drones were harassing the thing's head, and they seemed to be distracting it. At the very least, it had quit punching the hotel and was now swiping at the aerial annoyances.

Morrigan frowned at a new cluster of flying vehicles coming in from the west, taking a strange angle toward the thing. She muttered, "What the hell are they up to," then discovered the answer as they shot down the PDA drones. She swore, then swore again louder. "Someone's defending the damn beast with drones."

Scimitar reported, "It's a new set of signals, not connected to any of the others."

Demetrius growled, "Makes sense. *Somebody* created and sent this thing, right? I mean, it didn't crawl out of the sewers or something."

Ruby said, "Do what you can to get rid of them, even if it means hijacking the PDA drones. I'm sure you're better than their pilots."

Morrigan shot two down in quick succession with the EMP arrows Margrave had provided and managed to knock out another with a razor arrow. Then they swung around to the other side of the monstrosity, out of her range. "I'm starting to get a bad feeling about this."

Ruby replied, "Me too. Grentham, how long on the military?"

The dwarf sounded as worried as the rest of them. "We're at the base. Drones should be on-site in a couple of minutes, tops. Troops shortly after. Took a few to convince them we were legit."

Morrigan winced as a huge fist blasted a corner hotel room out of existence. "Tell them to hurry. I'm not sure how much longer we'll be able to distract it from taking down every casino in town."

Angelina Prash groaned as she pushed herself to her feet. "Damn dwarf. Damn Julianna Sloane. Damn stupid Magic City."

The babble in her earpiece distracted her. Then she interrupted the flow of orders and responses. "What the hell did you say? A giant crocodile on two legs? Show me." Her fight with the Aces jerk had broken the left lens of her smart glasses, but in the other, she saw a gigantic creature with a crocodile head stomping around outside. "Holy hell."

She knew in her bones that Sloane was behind it. *Somehow.* She'd realized the woman was crazy but had misjudged the magnitude of her damage. This was going too far. Angelina was fine with a little destruction, and her people had been under orders only to engage combatants. The monster was something else entirely and risked everyone, innocent and guilty alike.

She wrapped force magic around her shin to support the broken bone and downed her healing potion. The injury was severe enough that the single flask might or might not fully repair it, and she'd already used her other one. The continuing pain with each step suggested the magical splint was a wise choice.

She gathered the backpacks from her fallen escorts. They'd all brought explosives, blocks of C-4 to use if the need presented itself. They could use the bricks inside separately, or with a quick connection, turn the entire backpack into a bomb. She looped two over one shoulder and two over the other.

I get to the roof, and I throw one of these things into its mouth. Creature goes boom. I go on a vacation. No problem. She headed for the elevator, ordering her troops to disperse and go to wherever their alibis would claim they'd been that night if asked. Each of them offered to help her, but she refused assistance. "I've got this. Just get out."

Ruby screamed in alarm and ran as the tail suddenly lashed in her direction. A last-minute burst of force magic carried her over the thrashing appendage as it crashed into the wall of The Underground's casino section, caving it in. She whipped her sword down, slashing it against the thing's scales, and as before, accomplished nothing.

Morrigan said, "Oh," like she was surprised.

Ruby sighed and flipped her dirty hair out of her face. "What now?"

"It ran out of drones to fight. It's going back in for the hotel tower."

CHAPTER THIRTY

Ruby didn't climb the Crocosaur, despite Morrigan's suggestion that she should. Instead, she launched herself up to the roof of the casino level, which was still vibrating with the aftershocks of the thing's tail crashing into it. Deciding that staying there was neither safe nor useful, she blasted the surface beneath her with force magic, propelling her up beside the hotel tower. At the top of her flight, she grabbed a decorative ledge and pulled herself up onto it.

Using force magic, she dispatched lightning and explosive grenades at the thing, discovering that it was much harder to target its eye than she'd expected. She even tried smoke, but the monstrous creature didn't appear to care about any of them. The pipe Margrave had made for her concentrated her lightning into a cone that smashed into its face, which finally got a response. The beast raised a claw, scratched its jaw, and whipped out an arm at her position.

Only one option remained. Ruby used force magic to

blast herself off the building, holding her sword in two hands pointed straight ahead along her flight path. She rammed into the Crocosaur blade-first. Her artifact sword made a loud *squealing* sound as it penetrated the thing's skin and sank in to the hilt, leaving her hanging in midair by her grip on it. Unfortunately, the creature didn't notice she was there or considered her not worth addressing as it resumed its assault on the hotel tower in earnest.

The whole thing was starting to sway, and Ruby feared it didn't have long left. Unlike the Mist, which had collapsed in upon itself, she had a vision of the tower falling over into the casinos on either side of it. That would cause a cascade of damage.

She reached inside for the artifact and sent tendrils spiraling outward, growing in size as they went until they wrapped themselves around one of the giant arms. It yanked against their restraint, tore her away from her sword, and hurled her into the air. She released the tentacles and pushed them out again, grabbing at a spike on the thing's back. They found a hold and arrested her flight, and she used them almost like a tether to pull herself in. "Okay, I'm on its back. Now what?"

Morrigan replied, "Try to yank its head around and get its mouth open. I have one more explosive arrow. Maybe I can get it in there." As she said it, she knew the angle was all wrong. The thing had twisted away from her, and when it opened its mouth, the lower jaw didn't go down much. Instead, the upper jaw lifted toward the sky. She didn't have the correct line of attack, even if she sent the arrow in on an arc. "Repositioning."

She ran out into the hallway, turned right, and dashed to the end of the hall. One of Margrave's explosive discs made short work of a lock, and she kicked the door open and crossed to the window. "I have the best angle I can get. Let me know when you're ready." She pulled the arrow out of her quiver.

Idryll asked, "Anything I can do?"

Morrigan replied, "Don't get squashed."

"Great plan. I'm on it."

Ruby sounded like she was in pain as she said, "Getting hard to hold on here. Stupid thrashy monster. Tell me when you're ready."

Morrigan fitted the arrow to her bow, drew a deep breath, and aimed. "Okay, see if you can get the top of its mouth open."

<hr>

Ruby wrapped her arms around the spike on the Crocosaur's back as tightly as she could. Then she sent the tentacles spiraling out again, wishing for them to yank the thing's upper jaw upward. They looped behind another projection at the top of its head before continuing, presumably for leverage. Her interaction with the artifact was always strange, far less direct than her other magic. It took her commands but executed them in ways she wouldn't have considered. A moment later, power flowed out of her as the shadow tendrils jerked on its head. As she struggled to keep her hold, she growled, "Mo, do it."

An arrow sailed out of the nearby hotel, headed straight for the thing's open mouth. She lost sight of the projectile as it entered the maw, and a muffled detonation emerged. She lacked the energy to cheer. "Status?"

Morrigan's voice sounded like someone had stabbed her in the heart. "On target. It exploded in his mouth. He didn't seem to care."

Angelina Prash pushed open the door, finally gaining the roof of the casino. The structure swayed beneath her as she limped to the edge and looked down at the giant crocodile monster assaulting it. "Damn. You're an ugly one." She'd realized a few moments before that she was more wounded than she'd thought when her vision started to go double. *The dwarf must've broken something in my head.* It explained why her shin was still giving her problems. Much of the healing must have gone to repair the other damage.

That's fine. I only need to stay up long enough to get rid of this thing. Then I can portal out of here and get fixed up. She made it to the edge, armed one of the backpacks, and waited for her opportunity. Its mouth opened as it roared, apparently angry at the hotel for some reason, and she threw it. By the time it arrived, the jaws had snapped closed, and the explosives landed on its nose. The fierce detonation shattered windows all over the building, but the monster didn't seem injured, only irritated. It punched the tower again, and Angelina stumbled forward. The edge of the roof she stood on gave way, and she fell in the space.

She should've been terrified, but a clarity of purpose had settled over her. *This thing is going down, whatever it takes.* She said, "Need some drones," as she reached out with her magic, creating a line of force to grab at the base of a flagpole sticking out of the tower. The connection swung her to relative safety, and she got her feet established on a ledge. Two drones hovered nearby, courtesy of her team's infomancer. She attached a satchel charge to each and ordered, "Fly them into that thing's mouth."

Again, though, the giant crocodile monster refused to work with her. It closed its snout and batted the drones aside, and the satchels again failed to damage it. She only had two left, one in her hand and one on her back, and no idea how she would manage to hurt the creature with them.

Ruby looked upward to where the Worldspan woman was standing. "She's got some serious endurance."

Morrigan replied, "And a good plan, getting things down its throat, rather than only in its mouth. I don't see another way to get at anything vulnerable. Do you think you could yank it open again?"

"Yes. Probably. Assuming it doesn't throw me off, first." The thing was moving more abruptly now, hammering on the hotel tower. The cracking sounds coming from the building were getting more alarming with each passing second. "But your explosive arrows aren't going to do enough damage."

"Not that I have any left, anyway."

"Glam, have anything we can use?"

The tech replied, "No, but there are military drones ten seconds or so out. They just appeared on the Strip and are reacquiring control signals now."

"Scimitar, can you steal a couple?"

The infomancer didn't respond immediately. After seconds that felt like an eternity, her modulated voice came over the comms. "I have two. Fighting to keep ownership. Sending piloting control to D."

Demetrius said, "Got it. Okay, Jewel, what do you want me to do with them?"

"Ram one into the side of the thing and self-destruct it as a distraction, then shove the other down its throat."

"On it."

"I'll pull the mouth open again as soon as the first drone goes off."

Idryll asked, "Do you really think that's a good idea? Maybe leaving now would be the better choice."

Morrigan added, "Don't be stupid, Jewel. Try out smart instead for once. Get out of there."

Ruby shook her head. "I'm shielded. I'll be fine. I'm the backup plan in case the explosion doesn't cause it to open up enough."

"You're an idiot."

"Runs in the family, apparently."

Morrigan smiled at the joke, despite the insanity of the situation they faced. She held an arrow loosely in her hand, one of the two remaining. Right now, if the creature were explosive, she'd make her sister leave and blow it up, figuring that the damage would be less than what it was going to do if they didn't stop it. *That would be a tough decision to live with, so I guess I'm lucky it's not explosive.*

Military drones swooped in and sprayed bullets at the creature, who roared and thrashed as it tried to smash them out of the air. Two flew out of formation, one of them angling low at the thing's hips and the other circling toward its mouth. The distraction would probably be more effective higher up, but she silently applauded Demetrius's decision to keep the explosion as far from Ruby as it was reasonable to do.

As was so often the case, just when she thought things were going right, the tables turned. The Crocosaur slammed his fists into the hotel building, which gave a colossal shudder, and began to fall.

CHAPTER THIRTY-ONE

Ruby spotted the drone flying in toward the monster's mouth and shouted, "Okay, now." She slapped the energy capsule on her shoulder and poured all the power she had into the artifact, surrendering her will entirely to the task of making it yank the thing's mouth open.

The world went hazy as the tentacles ripped at the creature's jaw, and she concentrated only on that effort and on trying not to let her precarious grip on the spike fail. *Mental note. Add a low-open parachute to our gear.* The thing bellowed in anger as the tentacles pulled its head back, and it resisted, which opened its mouth exactly as she'd wanted.

Demetrius cursed loudly, and Scimitar's modulated voice said, "Lost ownership of the drones. Trying to reacquire." Ruby's spirits sank as she saw the drone that had been headed for the monster's mouth slew sideways. Then she noticed that what she'd taken for her movement was the hotel tower toppling to the left, toward Morrigan's location. She lost her grip on the spike and swung from the tentacles, which were loosening by the moment.

Morrigan's brain babbled meaningless words at the sight of the tower crumpling, and she hoped it wouldn't hit close enough or hard enough to bring the building she was in down. But her body had seized on a single thought. Her hands operated on autopilot as they brought the arrow to the bow and aimed more by instinct than by sight. She released the detonator projectile and watched as it crossed the distance to the drone that was supposed to be the distraction but was now hovering in place. It managed a glancing blow but hitting it wasn't the point.

The microwaves encountered the self-destruct mechanism in the drone, which was a standard part of all unmanned military craft, to prevent their capture and reuse by an enemy. The pulse activated the circuits that controlled it and sent their instructions a moment before they burned out. That signal caused the explosive core of the drone to detonate, which set off the bullets and rockets that made up its payload. The resulting fireball slammed into the Crocosaur, knocking it a step to the side and causing it to roar in fury.

Morrigan saw her sister swinging from the thrashing beast and launched herself into the air on a burst of force, heading right for the creature and praying that she'd find a way to reach Ruby before she fell.

Angelina Prash knew she was dead unless she did something drastic. Fortunately, the fear that realization normally would have caused was nothing compared to the sight of the gaping maw below her. She was moving before her mind registered the fact that she had a plan, leaping into the air toward the creature's mouth and slinging the satchel on her shoulder forward into her hands.

Idryll ground her teeth in frustration at the knowledge that she could do nothing to change the fight's outcome. It was the most frustrating moment of her life. *Once we get out of this, I'm going to protect the* hell *out of you, Ruby, whether you like it or not. Just, you know, don't die. I'm not ready to be part of the venamisha again quite yet.*

Ruby swung from the tentacles, which no longer had any leverage other than her body weight. That was as irrelevant to the Crocosaur as a fly would have been to her. Only one option remained. She let go of the thing's mouth, forcing the tentacles back into her arm with an effort of will and twisted as she fell into space.

She lined up the pipe with the wound the explosion had created in the creature's side and poured every ounce of remaining strength she had through it, blasting lightning into the single accessible vulnerable spot on its body. The monstrosity shuddered and screamed, throwing its head back in a defiant roar at the sky.

She'd seen Morrigan in the air before releasing the tentacles and fell in full confidence that her sister would keep her from splatting on the ground.

Morrigan grimaced and fired the grapnel on her arm at one of the military drones. It stabbed into the thing, and she used the connection as an anchor point to swing, detaching the line before she could pendulum back in the opposite direction. The move gave her enough momentum and distance to make her plan possible. She shouted, "Ruby, hold your breath," and created a portal beneath her sister, then dropped through the same rift a moment later.

Angelina Prash gave a satisfied smile as the creature's mouth gaped open. *Sometimes, things work out.* She cast three spells in quick succession. First, a force blast to send the satchel into the thing's throat since it had obligingly opened it up so wide she could drive an eighteen-wheeler down it. Second, a ball of lightning trailing after it so that the moment the explosives slowed from the impact, the electricity would trigger the detonator and set off all the C-4 in the backpack.

Finally, with regret that she wouldn't be able to see the results of her handiwork firsthand, Angelina cast a portal and plummeted through it.

Idryll watched Ruby and her sister wink out of existence, confident that Morrigan had matters well in hand. She had an excellent angle to see the figure dive off the falling building and toward the monster and saw an object fly out of its hands before it, too, vanished.

Then she had the distinct pleasure of seeing the Crocosaur shudder as something exploded inside it. It wavered, and Idryll ran for all she was worth to get out of the way of its falling form. Inside, though, she was laughing. *I knew life with Ruby would be exciting, but I had no idea how* exciting.

Morrigan hit the cold water with a gasp and swam for her sister, who was underwater a few feet away. Every smart person had a portal location over some kind of soft landing in case they needed it in an emergency. Hers was the massive Lake Mead, created by the Hoover Dam.

Ruby had surfaced and was laughing when she arrived, and Morrigan started laughing as well. Her sister splashed her, and she returned the favor immediately. Her comm crackled with Idryll's voice. "Are you two okay?"

Her sister replied, "Great. Having a relaxing swim. How are you?"

Morrigan snorted at Ruby's giddiness. The shapeshifter said, "Good. The thing blew up. You got its mouth open, and someone threw a bomb in there."

She asked, "And The Underground?"

Idryll replied, "Is going to need some serious reconstruction. The tower didn't hit anything else, so overall things are fine. Probably. I guess. I don't know anything about buildings."

Morrigan laughed as a wriggling creature rubbed against her leg. "Hey, Idryll. There are fish here."

"Bring me. Now."

Relieved laughter filled the comm channel as their allies, friends, and family joined the conversation.

Ruby said, "We won. Against a Crocosaur. Proving once again that Magic City will rise above every challenge the world can throw at it."

CHAPTER THIRTY-TWO

It took Julianna Sloane two days after the debacle in Magic City to realize she wouldn't be able to continue as she had been. Thompson was still under arrest, Smith was dead, and her plans to get the magicals back for what they'd done to her husband had come to nothing.

Her calls to the Carillos had gone unanswered. She had no doubt that they'd decided to cut ties with her. *Which is unfair since it was his witchy wife that had to be behind the monstrosity on the Strip. I knew they weren't the most rational people, but damn.* Inside, though, she admitted she should have anticipated working with them would result in disaster. *It's like Gabriel said. Negotiating from a bad position gets bad results.*

She snapped the clasps on her overnight case closed and put it with her other bags. A jet would be waiting at the airport to take her to Seattle and on to Canada. She'd live quietly for a while in a house on a lake they'd vacationed at once upon a time. When things were forgotten, a year or two tops, it would be time to come back and see what opportunities presented themselves.

Julianna had sent a bonus to Angelina Prash as thanks for keeping her desire for surgical destruction from turning into a complete obliteration of the city. The elf had responded by email, thanking her and informing her that Worldspan would no longer be available for hire. *I'll be getting a lot of that for a while, I imagine.*

A sound from the front of the apartment told her Stephens had arrived to escort her down to the car. She walked out of the bedroom and called, "My bags are in there. Take them down first."

An unfamiliar female voice replied, "Oh, I think not."

Julianna froze momentarily, then resumed walking down the short hallway into the living room. "You're not Stephens."

"No, I'm not." The voice belonged to a figure in black leather, with a mask that resembled the face of a dragon.

"You're one of the vigilantes from Magic City. Defenders. Heroes. Whatever it is you call yourselves."

The other person shrugged. "Citizen will do. Someone who cares about keeping the city safe from people who would do it harm. People like you, Mrs. Sloane."

She smiled. "You must be thinking of my husband. He was the one who did those things."

The other woman shook her head. "We have your records, Julianna. Scimitar was quite helpful. You should have treated her better."

She scowled. "Lies. All lies."

"We'll see. For the moment, though, I think you have another visitor."

The elevator doors opened to reveal Director Paul Andrews and several members of the PDA. Ruby had provided them with the information the infomancer had collected and had monitored their communications to know when they were coming. She'd wanted to be there for the event.

He said, "Julianna Sloane, you're under arrest."

She tried to protest, but he gave a tired head shake. "Don't care. Go peacefully, or they'll cuff you and do a perp walk for the media." He turned to the woman who'd been with him at the warehouse, tied up alongside him. "Get her out of here."

When they were gone, he put his hands on his hips and stared at Ruby. "So. Here we are."

"Yep."

"I still don't like your methods."

She laughed. "Mutual, Paulie. Mutual."

He nodded. "Fair enough. You won't have to deal with mine anymore. The department transferred me, thanks to my success in apprehending the Drow leading the anti-human movement in Ely. I'll deny it if asked, but whoever turned him in did me a favor and I know it. Anyway, this is the last time we'll see each other."

"Oh, I don't know. Maybe my friends and I will visit. Where are you headed?"

He smiled. "Somewhere you're not."

Ruby laughed again. "Understandable. If you decide you need a hand, you know where to find me."

"Not a chance."

"It's a weird world, Agent Andrews. Who knows, you might find yourself up against a Crocosaur."

His face twisted into a frown. "You're calling it a Crocosaur?"

Ruby sighed. "Everyone's a critic." Then she cast a veil and snuck away, departing through the same kitchen window she'd used to enter.

Elnyier walked into her office in Darkest Night with a scowl, still annoyed over the fact that persons unknown had invaded her privacy. She hadn't been able to get access to Dieneth to find out who it was. He was locked up in some sort of super maximum-security facility for magicals. It didn't take much thinking to deduce that it had to be the costumed vigilantes, though.

They'll get theirs. I'll let things quiet down a bit, then begin working on that little project. In the meantime, I need to start collecting dirt on the new Council members. She would refuse to leave her position as the Drow representative, no matter how much pressure the others put on her. She pulled her laptop out of the safe, took it to the desk, and sat. *First, it's time to move some money to my safety account quietly.*

She barely noticed the shimmer, but it was enough to catch her attention. When she looked up from the screen, two Drow women stood before her. The first was Shentia, a shopkeeper in the kemana and the source of several complaints about her leadership. "You, I know."

The other woman was unfamiliar. She was dressed all in tooled black leather, and her long white hair cascaded over one side of her chest in a thick warrior's braid. A sword hilt stuck up over her shoulder, and daggers rode at her hips. A bandolier across her chest held some sort of projectiles. "I don't know you."

That one replied, "Who I am isn't important. What is important is that you are going to leave Earth permanently, today. Right now, in fact. Should you return to this planet, your life will be forfeit."

She rose, throttling the anger that made her want to yell the words. "Who are you to give me orders?"

"Someone who knows what you've been up to."

"I refuse." She pressed the button hidden under the carpet with her toe. "You can't tell me what to do." Then she darted aside as two portals opened in her office, and the four guards from the room below, new ones who'd replaced those who had failed in their duty, dashed through them.

She'd expected surprise or shock and had hoped for fear on the part of the intruders. Shentia faded backward, pressing herself against the wall, which was satisfying. The other woman simply attacked. The sword scraped as it slid out of its scabbard, whistled as it whipped through the air, and made a strange, meaty sound as it separated the nearest guard's head from his body. Elnyier shrieked as it landed on her laptop and bounced off toward her.

The woman moved like water, spinning in the direction she'd cut and coming out of it throwing. Small darts sped across the room to bury themselves in the second guard's eyes as he triggered the pistol crossbow. A harsh wind blew the bolt away before it could get anywhere near the unknown woman.

That same wind grabbed the third guard and slammed him into the ceiling, then smashed him down to the floor with the sound of shattering bones. The fourth lifted his hands in fear, surrender, or simple survival instinct, but it didn't help him. The woman slid forward, barely seeming to expend any effort, and rammed the point of her sword through his throat. She held the lunge position for a moment before ripping the blade back out, spraying Elnyier with blood as she snapped it off her blade and returned the weapon to her scabbard.

Shentia stepped forward. "You were saying?"

Elnyier's eyes stayed locked on the white-haired warrior. "I know who you are. You're Kura-gari. The Shadow Blade." The other woman inclined her head in affirmation. She swallowed hard as all her plans fell into the abyss. "I'll go. Now. Like you said."

As the portal closed behind the former Council leader and Drow representative, Shentia said, "I think you scared the evil right out of her."

Nylotte gave a dark laugh. "It never works that way, unfortunately. Still, I'm sure substantial time will pass before she even thinks of coming back. If she does return, well, let me say it will be an absolute *pleasure* to see her again."

CHAPTER THIRTY-THREE

It was the first party Ruby had thrown since returning to Magic City. At college, she had hosted many, seeking to bring her human and magical friends together in a social setting. Her roommates had helped her prepare, and the house on the surface was full of happy people. The Desert Ghosts had provided the food, delivered by about a fourth of the club who showed up beforehand. Prex had promised that the rest would arrive eventually and that she should plan for the revelry to last until the next day.

She'd spent the days since bidding Julianna Sloane farewell in a haze of normalcy. She'd gone on another date with Demetrius and spent some time with her family. She'd also visited Oriceran to discuss with Nadar and the mystics how to make her time as *Mirra* truly matter. Tirina reported that the scholars were adapting, and though surly, had asked for permission to venture to the second set of towns.

Idryll had stayed close ever since the fight at The Underground and was still doing so tonight. At a different time in her life, the constant presence might have bothered Ruby. Right now, it was a reassurance that no matter how weird the future got, they'd be able to handle it together.

She circulated, making sure to connect with everyone she knew and introducing herself to those she didn't. She'd invited Alejo, but the sheriff had demurred. Ruby would show up on the woman's swing in disguise sometime soon to chat.

Diana Sheen and her people had been encouraged to attend as well, but none had yet arrived. Ruby had the impression they wouldn't be coming, that something was up with what Diana had referred to as their "command hierarchy." She hoped she hadn't caused trouble for the group. That thought made her think of Rath, and she laughed at her mental image of the mischievous troll.

Margrave was busy arguing with Morrigan over who made the best Captain Kirk. Her sister was a big fan of Chris Pine, and Margrave wasn't budging on his position that Shatner was, and would always be, the only true James Tiberius. She grinned at them in passing but didn't interrupt.

A soft touch took the can of Coke out of her hand and replaced it with a pint glass of beer. Abbot Thomas said, "We made this one special for you. Give it a try."

She did and frowned at the fruity taste that hovered around the edges. "I almost recognize it, but not quite."

He grinned. "It's dragon fruit."

She blinked in surprise, then laughed. "How appropriate."

"As you kids today say, 'I know, right?'"

Ruby broke into laughter and shook her head. "You're awesome. You know that?"

He nodded serenely. "I do."

The rest of the evening passed in a blur of enjoyment, and at around three in the morning, the only people left were the residents of the house and a handful of Desert Ghosts who steadfastly refused to go home. Demetrius patted her arm and said, "I'm going upstairs. Join me?"

She replied, "In a minute or two," and walked outside and sat on the steps.

Her companion sat beside her. "What's next?"

"I think the day-to-day of Magic City's defense is under control with Morrigan and Demetrius on the job. Elnyier isn't obstructing the Council anymore so that situation should resolve. The families are still shell-shocked, but I think most will rally and choose to rebuild. It's probably time we went to Oriceran and spent some time getting a handle on the whole leading-the-Mist-Elves thing."

"Sounds boring."

Ruby laughed. "Well, we should probably keep our hand in, just a little, so we don't get rusty. I'm guessing Diana's team might have some tasks they can outsource from time to time. Plus, it's not like we can't portal back whenever to check on things, or if there's trouble."

The shapeshifter grinned. "Now you're talking."

"For what it's worth, I couldn't be happier with my choice of companion."

Idryll gave a regal nod. "Of course. I'm glad I chose not to kill you back then."

She turned to face her partner with a wide smile. "Chose, is it? That's not quite how I remember it."

"Well, you've been hit on the head a lot. Your memory probably isn't what it used to be."

The argument that followed was as entertaining as it was irrelevant. When Ruby crawled into bed with Demetrius later that night, it was with a profound sense that, *finally*, Magic City was safe, and her life was heading in the proper direction. *Of one thing, I'm sure. With friends like Idryll around, it'll never be boring.*

Diane, Rath and the Federal Agents of Magic popped up in this series. While this series is ending, their story does not. Join the intrepid Federal Agents of Magic in the next series ROGUE AGENTS OF MAGIC and book one, *ROGUE OPS*.

Thank you for reading the final installment of the Magic City Chronicles, and for continuing on to read these author notes!

I can't believe this series is over. After living with Ruby and her crew for the last eight months, it's hard to imagine leaving her behind. I really enjoyed her character arc, which led in ways I didn't expect at the beginning. The way that each series, and the characters within them, take on lives of their own is a huge part of the reward of writing for me.

Reminder from last month - I'm headed to Vegas for the 20Books show in November and will be around for the author signing event on Friday. If you're going to be around, let me know, I'd love to say hi!

The first Rogue Agents of Magic book will be titled, appropriately, *Rogue Ops*. I expect that series to be harder-edged in the same way FAM was as compared to those that followed. More wicked tactics in the fights, slightly more colorful language, and, of course, more troll! Now that

Rath has become more or less the equal of the other agents in fighting prowess, he'll be mixing it up with even more enthusiasm than in the past.

I have now seen *Cruella* five times. Five. And I'm still enjoying it. I know there are some haters out there, but I'm definitely not one of them. Looking forward to *Black Widow* this week.

Totally digging *Loki*. Rewatching *Castlevania* with more intentionality; the plot makes a lot more sense when you remember what happened in the last episode. Imagine, right? Going slowly on *Discovery*.

I read a thing today about "languishing." It's described as a mental condition that's not quite depression and not quite ennui, but somewhere in between. Like life has just worn you out, and you're not finding joy as often as before. I'm feeling this at the moment. Starting to come out of it, but it's an uphill climb. Apparently, it's an entirely normal response to the experience we've all shared of COVID and quarantine over the last year.

It reminds me to treasure the happy bits just a little more than I might otherwise do.

My wife spent most of quarantine devoting lots of time to *Animal Crossing: New Horizons*. We just bought the game again, on a different device, so she can start a second island. That's exactly the sort of thing I would do, so I respect it. Two years ago, I was all about Sim City, and had 3 different accounts going so I could feed materials from one to the other. Then I had to stop playing that because it was keeping me from, you know, working and stuff.

Reminder again - If you're not part of the Oriceran Fans Facebook group, join! There's a pizza giveaway every month, and Martha and (usually) I and all sort of fun author folks show up via Zoom to chat with our readers. It's a great time, and the community feel to it is truly fantastic. Oriceran Fans. Facebook. Your phone is probably within reach. Do it!

Before I go, once again, if this series is your first taste of my Urban Fantasy, look for "Magic Ops." I promise you'll enjoy it, and you'll get more of Diana, Rath, and company. You might also enjoy my science fiction work. All my writing is filled with action, snark, and villains who think they're heroes. Drop by www.trcameron.com and take a look!

Until next time, Joys upon joys to you and yours – so may it be.

PS: If you'd like to chat with me, here's the place. I check in daily or more: https://www.facebook.com/AuthorTRCameron. Often I put up interesting and/or silly content there, as well. For more info on my books, and to join my reader's group, please visit www.trcameron.com.

If you enjoyed this book, please consider leaving a review. Thanks!

Here we are at the end of another great series – Magic City Chronicles – in the Oriceran Universe. We'll miss Ruby and Idryll and all the others.

But sometimes great stories come back around and because you guys, the Fans kept saying you wanted to see Diana and that troll, Rath again… Well, we listened.

Remember Federal Agents of Magic? Coming back on September 21st is Part Two in the exciting and fun story as Rogue Agents of Magic.

Don't worry, the whole team is back, including Kayleigh and Cara but this time they're working outside the law. They've been falsely charged and disavowed and some hope they turn tail and run. But we don't write the kind of books where the hero gives up.

We write the kind where the heroes run toward trouble, accompanied by their ride or die friends. Kind of like our own A-Team. For any millennials or Generation Z reading this – look that old TV series up. It was a good one.

You remember that old saying about 'write what you know'? I've been doing this writing thing in various forms for over 30 years now. A helluva long time. What that cliché means to me is that who we are as people comes across in our writing whether we like it or not.

Basically optimistic? The characters will be solution oriented. Don't really care for humanity? There will probably be a lot of side comments that tear down others in small or big ways.

There's a lot of that latter style of writing out there. I find it grating on the soul over time and unnecessary.

Michael and myself – and TR Cameron – share that quality. We believe that almost everyone in this world wants to get along with others. They want the world to function in a way that brings the most good to others. And that small percentage out to do harm? Those are the bad guys and we blow them up in our stories. In real life, we recognize a bad guy for who they are and move on. Life is too short to shake your fist for very long. I do that and I ignore all the good people around me. Seems counter-productive.

So, enjoy this last dance with Ruby and her friends and get ready for something new and yet, familiar. It's like the next phase of Oriceran. The Universe has been around now for four years and has created almost 200 books and so many great characters. Time to bring some back for another visit. Hold on, it's gonna be a fun ride. More adventures to follow.

JOIN THE ORICERAN UNIVERSE FAN GROUP ON FACEBOOK!

https://www.instagram.com/lmbpn_publishing/

https://www.bookbub.com/authors/michael-anderle